The Key-Stone of the Bridge

Craig Meggy

3rd Edition

ACKNOWLEDGMENTS

All the characters in this tale are completely fictitious but Ben Alder Bothy
and the adjacent hills are not.
As for the legends that surround this yarn, you can decide.

Thanks to Ash for the cover photograph.

1 THE BOTHY

I woke from the same dream I'd had so many times before. One in which I seemed to be tethered in some way to a bus, hurtling along a winding road that clung to a steep mountainside. I would be flying high above, swooping and wheeling, sometime almost landing on the roof. Then the bus would swerve around another corner, and off I would soar. It always felt as though I could control my flight, and yet somehow I never did; nor did I ever land.

Drowsy and slightly numb as the dream faded, I relaxed and looked out of the oval window. The familiar lights and sights of Edinburgh loomed through the clouds, a picture-postcard grid of Georgian architecture, splendor fleetingly revealed.

As groups of raindrops raced across the window, and runway lights pricked the gloom, the flight attendants took their seats. A heavy bounce, a chorus of stifled gasps and we all braced until the rising crescendo of hydraulic forces fighting air and tarmac gradually eased. Slowing to a roll, we taxied gently to the gate, relieved as the throbbing roar of the engines subsided.

"Welcome to Edinborrow Airport, please remain seated…" the American flight attendant launched into her practiced spiel, mangling the name of the city then culminating cheerfully with, "And safe onward travel if Edinborrow is not your final destination."

Aye, well, whatever you want to call it, it wasn't my final destination. Me, I was on a mission, to reunite with old friends and head north to a remote mountain shelter in the Highlands of Scotland. It was there, we would gather as we had done many times before, but on this occasion, to honour a request written in the last will and testament of one John Brown, or as he was better known to us, "Banjo". At the time, I had no idea this weekend in tribute to our departed friend would have such a bizarre outcome.

Now, as we scorched that wet tarmac, one of my companions on this quest, Craig 'Doc' Docherty – mechanic, former drug dealer and petty criminal – had been getting creative. First, he had run a line of epoxy resin methodically around the top of a beer can bearing the legend, 'McEwans Export'. Then, with the precision of a craftsman he had brought together the serrated edges, made when a hacksaw had dissected the flimsy aluminum cylinder. After testing the repair by gently twisting the top, he placed the modified can in a plastic bag, carefully packing it away before heading for the airport. Twenty-seven minutes later, he stood fidgeting in the waiting area, impatiently scanning the arrivals board and shooting furtive glances at the uniformed security guard. We would all find out soon enough what it was the wee nutcase had been up to.

I grabbed my bag; we needed to get going to maximise the light of a fleeting winter sun, and it was already 7.30 a.m. As a pneumatic hiss heralded the opening of the doors, Doc was revealed. Wee pugilist's nose and that stocky frame, a consequence of several generations of West Coast inbreeding, all wrapped up in grime and smelling like burnt rubber and axel grease. The last time I had seen him 'scrubbed up' was at his own wedding; he had turned up in a kilt: we had half expected he would just wash his coveralls. Now there he stood, clad head to toe in black, and as usual, scowling.

"Alright Doc, how's you?" I greeted him cheerfully, and smiled at the sight of that familiar visage and at the zone of exclusion that had formed around him like penicillin on a petri dish, as those waiting for other passengers kept a discrete distance.

The reply in a Glasgow brogue rattled out in a staccato growl. "Aye great, Scully, fuckin' great, how's you?"

He frowned up at me myopically, squinted his beady brown eyes under that brow of faded scars and with a wry smile, grabbed my outstretched hand.

"Shite, ah slept about an hour, I'm knackered," I stifled a yawn then added, "Hey, but the wee stewardess was an absolute doll; red hair, green eyes, my favourite color scheme…"

"Oh fer fuck sake, Scully," Doc ignored the cheerful rejoinder, "Stop yer moaning, man, it's a three-hour drive. You can kip in the van. Now, c'mon, let's get the fuck out of here; rent-a-cop is giving me the evil eye."

As usual, Doc liberally peppered his every utterance with 'fuck' as if the word itself was punctuation. A quick glance confirmed my suspicion: The guard looked about fourteen years old.

"Aye well," I winked at Doc, "I reckon its your dark ambience that's making him nervous, and aye, here it's good to see you an' all, you old bastard!"

As the exit doors opened, our welcoming party was revealed, icy raindrops turned fleetingly into dancing marionettes in puddles sporting small flotillas of cigarette butts. I pulled on a woollen hat and darted to the safe cover of the parking garage. Doc waved his keys at a black Vauxhall Combi Van. It responded with a cheerful two-tone beep.

"Aye so, did you get everything okay?" I asked with some concern. Doc merely opened the back doors to reveal boxes of food and items of hiking gear in a jumbled heap. My old Lowe Alpine backpack retrieved from a dusty attic looked non the worse for wear.

"Good man! Oh, and here, this better ride up front with us!" I held up a bag emblazoned with the words, 'Duty Free'.

"Ohh yah fuckin' dancer," Doc licked his lips as he inspected the label on the whisky bottle. "*Nectar!* Oh… an' here, yer ma' said," he paused and then in an attempted imitation of an elderly females voice comically changed the pitch of his thick guttural brogue, "Now, you boys be careful! You're not so young anymore!"

"Tsk… I snorted, "forty-seven but still someone's wee laddie eh? It's no' like we're going to the North Pole! Anyway here, how's Susie and those bonnie wee bairns of yours?"

"Whit the mean-agers!"

"Mean-agers?"

"Aye, all they do is pout and whine unless they want money, then they're my wee darlings again,"

"Dinnae give them money so often then!"

"Aye right, Scully, great advice. Here, how's Angie?"

"Oh aye good, good, grand! Aye things are grand!"

As Doc paid for parking I examined my somewhat dishevcled reflection in the side mirror. Long brown hair flecked with grey tied in a ponytail, a stubbly angular chin, and a beaky nose framed by a pair of tired looking green eyes stared vacantly back. I rubbed my face vigorously to slough off dead skin cells and sleep, then pulled off my hat, smoothed back my hair, and smiled happily as I recalled a previous trek. On that occasion, Banjo had gently drawn a wide-open eye on our friend Donald's forehead as he slept, passed out in a stupor. He had spent the entire trip like that including the train ride home.

"What the fuck are you grinning at?" Doc had re-appeared.

"Acht… the time Banjo drew that eyeball on Donald's napper?"

"Oh aye, wee fat Doughboy wasnae happy about that!"

These days Donald Dougherty actually hated being called 'Doughboy' but not as much as he detested being referred to as wee and fat. As Doc and Donald always engaged in a friendly rivalry involving a degree of not so-subtle-verbal jousting, Doc used the nickname and those particular adjectives whenever he could. It was actually a bit of a cheek coming from Doc who did not exactly tower over Donald; to me they both looked about 5'8", maybe 5'9" in a flattering light. In fact, I reckoned Doc's fondness for the 70s and 80s probably wasn't only for the music: Platform boots were one fashion item only he missed. Mind you, he could also lose a pound or two, but then 'slightly shorter chubbier' Doughboy really did not trip off the tongue with the same cachet.

We peeled out of the airport and headed north. Doc braked sharply at each speed camera then accelerated as soon as we passed the chevrons. Persistent icy rain lashed the windscreen and as he held the wheel in one hand he began digging absentmindedly in each nostril.

"Here, you no' eaten yet?" I laughed

"Acht, get ti fuck just looking for a wee snack, eh… we'll stop at the Grill, aye?"

"Aye couple of hours though!"

"Long time and long way ti come for you but *it is* good ti be heading back, eh?"

The tone of Doc's voice had changed to a pitch that actually suggested enthusiasm. Well, of course he was up for this, we were heading back to what might best be described as a judgment-free zone, at least as far as drinking and swearing were concerned. Just four old friends, totally isolated in a mountain shelter, way off the grid with no creature comforts but a wood-burning stove and the whisky in our packs.

"Aye, it's been a few years Doc but fine reason for lacing up the boots again. A final request is a job worth doing. Em… talking of which did you remember the plaque?"

A silly question, Doc would not have forgotten something so important.

"Eh… aye," Doc frowned clearly irritated that I had questioned his abilities, "Everything is safely packed away, I got a nice wee brass number, opted for nails 'bout three inches long, round tops so they'll go in flush. Figure maybe we might even be able ti drive 'em through then bend the ends over. I'm no' actually that worried though, I mean who the fuck would nick something like that, eh…?"

"Aye well, there's always some arsehole who thinks they're being funny!"

I moved swiftly to another concern: The status of our destination.

"Here, eh… have you heard any news, is it still standing, it no' been burnt down has it?"

"Oh aye, it's still there," Doc paused and qualified his assertion, "Well, I heard a report last year from a couple of boys climbing Ben Alder, took shelter, said it was a mess, but roof still intact. Fuck, Scully, it's well built, it'll probably last another hundred years!"

"Aye true, very true."

"Eh… spoke ti young Robbie last weekend!"

"How's he doing?"

"Getting the train at eight, wi' Doughboy as agreed."

"Good stuff, an' how is the young pup?"

Robbie Barclay was easy as the youngest and newest member of this assembly; his place in the pecking order and brunt of many a joke was set in stone. He was also the only one of us without a *bona fide* nickname, a Scottish badge often awarded for a youthful act of breathtaking stupidity or a prominent physical characteristic. Usually though, it was a modified surname as useful for rapid communication on the football field as it was for confusing the forces of flaw and disorder.

"Eh… aye, okay." Doc sounded hesitant.

"Aye, it's been over a year," I scratched my head and recalled the last time and place, "Curry, Christmas a year back!" We'd had a drunken conversation in which he had extolled the virtues of his job as a ranger in the Pentland Hills park but complained about the isolation of his accommodation. "Here are him n' Sarah still out in the boonies?"

"Eh, aye, Carlops," Doc scowled and chewed his lower lip, "Last time I saw him was when we met for a couple of pints, ti tell him 'bout this little jaunt. Ended up a no' bad night n' all, few beers, Robbie back on the last bus eh… just. I've no' seen him since!"

"I'm no' surprised. Sarah probably hasnae let him back out the house, here though, that's no' exactly a wild night by some standards, eh?"

"Aye…" Doc exhaled.

He had reluctantly moved to Edinburgh in his early twenties, fearing its reputation for standoffish behavior. However, his life in Glasgow was being complicated both by the police and his dodgy business competitors. So he moved East and found work in a garage that actually preferred to put cars back together, then quickly located the liveliest bars and in due course many a wild night in the company of myself, Donald and Banjo. Much to his surprise he also discovered there was considerable joy to be had in our other favorite activity, usually instigated by Banjo. Now hiking up down and across Scotland's heatherclad mountains was something Doc had last done reluctantly as a youth in the Boys' Brigade. However, as he often pointed out, in those days, he did not get to reward all that physical activity with several pints of beer.

"Acht," Doc exhaled this time sharply while gripping the steering wheel hard, his shoulders hunched and almost hid his neck. "Fer fuck Scully, listen, I was in the Tass, couple of weeks back, was at the bar when I spotted Sarah in the snug, looking a bit intense wi' some bloke, holding his hand staring deep into his eyes, you get the picture?"

"What naw really?" I paused and considered this news, a monotonous metronome beat from the windscreen wipers filled the silence, "eh… have you said anything to Robbie?"

"Eh no, no' had the chance just waiting for the right moment I didnae feel much like tellin' him by phone, thought it would be better eh…"

"Did you recognise the bloke?"

"Naw, never seen him before in my puff, the next time I was up at the bar they'd gone. *Fuck* why did she have ti come inti the Tass, could she no' have done that in some other pub?"

"Aye, very inconvenient for you!" Typical of Doc I thought, laughing at the misfortune of strangers or even the stupidity of friends; not a problem. However, telling a friend some unpleasant news was not a task he relished: It required empathy. Doc needed a drink in him for that. "Here, doesnae seem like her though, I thought they were pretty happy!"

"Aye well, people change maybe it'll no' come as a surprise, who knows eh…? Could be why he wanted ti come along, take a break!"

"Aye could be."

"Well he was *very* keen to come but then he was good friends wi' Banjo as well."

"Acht, anyone who liked a drink was good friends with Banjo! Anyway we *all* want to say goodbye, that's why we're here!"

"It might also be the pretty picture I painted as I reminisced wi' my whisky-tinted specs on." Doc flashed his trademark evil grin eyes firmly on the road.

"Aye, did you tell him what to expect with the lack of mod cons and the weather? Oh, and here, you did tell him about the ghost didn't you?" I grinned, I knew what the response to that would be.

"Acht, fer fuck sake Scully, *ghost*, that's just a stupid story!" He shook his head glowered then shot me a sideways glance as if he suspected I was winding him up. "Anyway, he's been out on the hills before, he was in the army, he'll cope!"

"Here, he's been out the army for ten year, '92 was it no'?"

"Aye, well, he tromps the hills every day wi' his job, *and* he's no' even forty yet? Now that old bastard Doughboy well he was more reluctant!"

"Aye, well so was I, travel in the winter can be a hassle but there was *no way* I was leaving you to do this alone."

"Aye, well, fat boy grumped a wee bit more so I resorted ti some low blows ti persuade the wee fucker."

"Aye, like what?"

"Well, I called and suggested maybe he was getting older, fatter an even softer on his island paradise, but I think it was posting the knitting patterns for the nice wee fluffy woolly number that clinched it!"

"Aye, nice one!" I chuckled as an image of Donald's irate face as he opened his mail formed. In fact, we found out later that neither, the inference that he would rather stay home knitting or the phone messages had actually had a direct bearing upon Donald's decision. They had, however, spurred him to go dig out his photo album, pour himself a large dram of fifteen-year-old malt, flick through the pages and fondly reminisce. The following morning found him in his attic dusting off and checking out his gear.

"Here, what time is it?"

"Just after the hour!"

Doc jabbed a button on the radio and growled, "weather" by way of explanation. Unsurprisingly, for January 27th the forecast was not great, low pressure with rain turning to snow over higher ground.

Two hours later, we pulled into the Ballinluig Motor Grill, a favourite café, ramshackle and faded with a flickering neon sign that read 'Open,' and an aroma of burnt grease and diesel oil.

The increase in altitude had turned the icy rain to fat flakes of snow that swirled silently into the soft colorless light of a Highland dawn.

Waking myself, I unfolded my lanky frame and climbed groggily out of the van. Doc charged off to get out the cold. I slouched behind scuffed my shoes through the dusting of snow.

We had consumed two breakfast platters, each replete with grilled sausage, bacon, mushrooms, baked beans, toast and a sunny fried egg, in record time. Back on the road, I optimistically attempted to find a more favorable weather report. The futility of this action was compounded by the remoteness of the road; we strained to hear Radio Scotland through static crackle and undulating reception.

"Ah, fuck this for a game, Scully, get ah... '*Let it Bleed*' on!" Doc barked out the request for this, his favorite and in his considered and totally unbiased opinion, the finest Rolling Stones album of all time. Moments later the distinctive tremolo notes and rhythmical rattle of the guiro resonated from the speakers and seemed to fill the vans interior like slowly rising water. Right on cue, we joined in and loudly sang almost in tune with

'Gimme Shelter' as we rhythmically bopped our heads, tapped feet or drummed on the dashboard. Doc threw the van around one corner after another undaunted by a close shave with a Toyota Land Cruiser towing bales of wet hay, eyes on the road foot firmly on the pedal. Meanwhile various items in the rear of the van danced and rattled from side to side, an accompanying percussionist of dubious talent for Mick n' Keith.

We hurtled through Kinlochrannoch, its main street deserted save for a local lassie. Her physique severely tested the fabric of a pair of stretch jeans as she puffed on a cigarette and pulled a mangey looking dog from one fascinating-smelling lamppost to the next.

On we drove until the fading falsetto tones of the London Bach Choir heralded the end of the final song, as the notes resonated we pulled off the road onto a frozen heavily rutted forest track. Sliding the door open, Doc hauled out his pack and threw his baseball cap in the van. He quickly concealed his shaven head and its bald crown with a green and white woollen beanie, carefully tucking in each of his oversized ears. I wasted no time and swapped my travel clothes for sea-green leggings and donned a fleece shirt in Black Watch tartan, as well as my tried and trusted sapphire blue rainproof jacket. After lacing up heavy boots and strapping on gaiters, I grabbed my own pack and hauled it out the van with a visceral grunt.

Our mood was grim and businesslike as we swiftly prepared for the trek. Backpacks filled with food and clothes, the PVC reservoirs of CamelBaks filled with water, plastic bottles and hipflasks with duty-free whisky. Finally, four half-litre cans of McEwans Export were shoved into the top and side pockets of each pack. That left a few cans, so Doc slipped his finger under a ring-pull, lips pursed, stubble-coated chin contorted into a grimace of anticipation.

'Pstttt!' the sound of a liberated beer reverberated through the snowy silence of the forest.

"Oooo, an Eccy for breaky, or is it brunch?"

"Oh fer fuck sake, Scully," Doc groaned, "Yer puns are getting worse!"

We quickly dispatched the beer, chased with a belly-warming slug of single malt whisky, fuel for the long, hard slog ahead over nine miles of boggy half-frozen ground. Then we groaned, swore and staggered, arched under the unfamiliar weight of packs that would swiftly chafe our shoulders as the stiff-legged march began. Heavy footsteps in rigid boots crunched and cracked icy puddles, all in perfect time with the gentle creaks and sloshing sounds from the liquid portion of our cargo.

Five miles of resolute trudging later, we arrived at a small wooden lodge. Locked and shuttered, it had an outside bench under the cover that faced the dark waters of Loch Ericht. We eased our packs off, stretched our aching backs and grumbled rhetorically. To the north, a snow-covered panorama of towering mountains stretched into the low cloud. The dim light and heavy sky gave the color and contrast of a black and white photograph. In this light, even the patches of green provided by the uniform square plantations of non-native Sitka spruce appeared black.

As we leaned on the low balustrade, Doc lit a cigarette, the metallic click from his lighter seemed the loudest sound for miles around. He stared silently east at the horizon and the town of Dalwhinnie. Hidden from sight some eighteen miles in the distance, the pagoda roof of its distillery sheltered a stash of dust-frosted barrels of whisky.

I had been busy sniffing the rank smell coming from beneath my shirt when Doc offered me one. "Oh, ta' here… thought you might have given up?"

"Aye, well I had, but ho, it's a special weekend," Doc exhaled a plume of smoke into the cold air and added, "Did you hear Maggie got a job an' moved ti London then?"

Banjo's sister had taken his death badly, but as the pain had faded we'd regained our status as pseudo-older brothers and now received sporadic updates of significant developments in her life.

"Aye I'd heard, that's the beauty of e-mail; well, in addition to oddly-worded notes from Nigerian gentlemen and links to dodgy websites. Here, where was it you saw her?"

"Aye, ah was in town, bumped into her and ehm… Paula Burns, we went inti the Green Mantel for a quick pint. By the way, *that* was when she told me that *this*," Doc paused and pointed a finger at a cloud cloaked mountain, "had been Banjo's the last request!"

"She took her time, eh? No' that I blame her!"

"Aye, 'parently her n' her Ma were finally sorting through his stuff, an they found an old photo of us lot. That was the trigger; she recalled what had been writ in his will."

"I never even knew he'd made a will; what did he have to leave?"

"She didnae say if there was any money; it was a council house, bike was totaled, that was really all he had. I asked about his boots and gear but they'd gone ti charity along wi his books and CDs."

"Aye, well, in with nowt out the same way! You know, he'd never mentioned it to me, but he totally loved it here! Most years we'd be trudging out knackered, cold and hungover and he'd already be planning the next year!"

"Aye, that was him right enough, never mentioned it ti me either but eh, kind of a morbid topic for *that* happy-go-lucky bampot!"

"Aye true, very true!" I nodded enthusiastically. Banjo's ability to always look on the bright side of life had been legendary. If Maggie and their mother hadn't made the arrangements for his funeral service, the Monty Python ditty of that name would certainly have blasted out the speakers as the coffin slid through the doors into the furnace.

"Here Scully do *you* remember Paula... Paula Burns, used to drink in Nicky Tams?"

"Err might do, hard to say, give us a clue?" I searched the distant smoky haze of my youth but the name wasn't ringing any bells.

"Blonde lass, always wore yon skin tight leather pants, think she went by the name Bunny."

"Oh, Bunny, was her name Paula? Heh, well now I remember, aye here if I close my eyes I can still see that pert wee arse of hers in those leather pants. What a glorious sight!"

"Fuck aye, mind Banjo trying ti get his leg over wi' her at Irish Tony's?"

"Indeed, a sterling effort, oh... and here that was some party!"

The soiree in question had actually been an epic even by our high standards. It had culminated in several arrests after complaints regarding the noise emanating from a stereo system apparently borrowed from the main stage at Glastonbury. After several visits and terse requests to 'turn it down,' the boys in blue just confiscated the stereo. The arrests commenced after the entertainment had turned to one of our biker friends doing 'donuts' in the front room on a Triumph Bonneville. Incarcerations continued apace as the stereo-deprived drunken horde began a tunelessly litany of 70's and 80's 'classics' with the windows now wide open to allow dispersal of the exhaust fumes. I will remember the sight and sound of that police van rocking from side to side as the 'Middle of the Road' classic, 'Chirpy Chirpy Cheep Cheep' echoed into the warm Edinburgh night almost as fondly as the more tuneful version that featured Sally Carr's hotpant-clad, seemingly endless and unbelievable smooth legs.

A deep, dirty laugh rumbled out as Doc continued, "Ho ho, tell you what Scully, wee bit more cowhide needed for that job these days!"

"Really? Aww, she was such a slim wee thing!"

"Aye well, the Bunny I bumped into looked like she might have eaten the Bunny you remember, she asked after *you* n' all."

"Really?" I stood up a little straighter at this news, my chest thrust out like a peacock, "Well, she *was* gorgeous an' all! So, what did she say then, 'Hey Doc, where's that well hung, good looking mate of yours these days?'"

"No' quite," He paused to spit a gob of phlegm into the snow, "All she said was to say 'Hi,' eh... she actually used the term 'nutter'."

As a gust of wind shifted the clouds like the lifting of a veil, the top and northern flank of Ben Alder was dramatically revealed. A stand of old-growth pines was thrown into perspective, their prominence severely diminished by the massive bulk of the mountain. It squatted like a speckled whale, its broad back sloping gently towards the north, its huge head a rocky outcrop.

"Aye there she is."

"Aye but no' for long," Doc grabbed his pack just as the clouds sluggishly drifted back and shrouded the summit once more. "Changeable as ever, better fuckin' shift it eh?"

We made good progress at first, the freezing conditions of the night before had put a firm icy crust on the muddy path. However, as we reached a Sitka spruce plantation, we found that small rivers now funneled down the hillside between each regimented row. The cursing and stumbling commenced as we tried to pick a route that avoided the half-frozen quagmire. It quickly became a monotonous slog a struggle that went on for what felt like hours. Slipping, sinking, swearing, all while we cherished the thought that once past this manmade obstacle, the path would climb away from the atrocious bog mire.

"Fuck," Doc exclaimed in an anguished howl bent over, exhausted, hands on knees, "Sitting on my arse watching TV maybe wasnae the best preparation for this; I am knackered!"

"Aye c'mon last mile, dig in, think of warm soup and whisky," I shouted the encouragement breathlessly while I struggled to extricate one of my boot from the sticky grasp of half-frozen mud.

"Aye, what about dry socks and a blow job?"

"Aye fer fuck sake I meant to say, Heidi Klum called me yesterday said if she could get a sitter, she'd meet us there!"

"Oh ho, *nice* one" Doc deadpanned his retort through gritted teeth, "Here, hope she remembers my socks!"

It felt like an eternity until to our huge relief, a steep climb finally led us onto a path that became firmer and the brutal slog relented. One last dig into the reserves past a peat bog, across some rock-strewn ground and we reached a copse of mature Scots pine. To our left a red deer stag, a ten-pointer, stood frozen, his magnificent crown of antlers turned towards us as he sniffed the air regally like a Monarch of the Glen. A gust of wind carried the rank smell of sweat and cigarettes to his nostrils and he bolted, followed eagerly by a group of startled hinds; they paused on the ridge, silhouettes against the snowy backdrop.

We just stood there side by side and silently contemplated the view. As we caught our breath, our chests heaved in synchrony with the gentle creaks as the wind moved the ancient pines. Our gaze held fast on the remote glen before us, gouged by a massive prehistoric glacier, it swept and soared from distant peaks to the shores of Ben Alder Bay.

There on its far side nestled into the foot of the mountain from which is rugged ramparts had been quarried, resolute against the countless storms and incessant rain, stood our destination.

The darkened granite walls and snow coated roof of an isolated mountain hut known as Ben Alder Bothy.

2 WHISPERLITE

The weathered walls of the Bothy rose to about seven feet and met a slate roof that sagged slightly at one end. No light shone from two small windows embedded in the western façade; they just seemed to stare at the world like soulless eyes. The guttering, eaten by rust, had long since fallen off and allowed the persistent rain to carve a deep groove in the peaty soil like a tiny moat around a castle. At each apex, the gable ends were finished off with a stone chimney, one topped by a cracked clay pot, time and the winter storms had dealt with the other.

The only splash of color was provided by a dark blue wooden porch, which allowed the main door to be set to the right, facing away from the prevailing wind that could whip down the Glen. Over the door, someone at some point in the past had fixed the skull of a red deer stag. Its empty eye sockets and missing teeth seemed to befit the spartan accommodation it now stood guard over.

We stood and watched the Bothy carefully for signs of life: smoke coming from the chimney or others headed out to gather wood, but there was no one there. It was dark and empty, a solitary outpost of civilization eclipsed by a surrounding domain carved by ancient geological forces, its sole companion a lone leaf-bare ash tree.

Spurred on by the sight of the Bothy uninhabited with roof intact, we bounded down the hillside. Our limbs ached and we cursed and groaned as we hoisted our heavy packs up steep steps across a wooden bridge high above the roaring torrent. Then after crossing a short stretch of moor we splashed through the shallow and half-frozen waters of a second, smaller river and eagerly climbed the last few steps to the Bothy door.

On the door, a rusty horseshoe hung above a circular white metal plaque that simply declared "M.B.A." then all in uppercase the statement.

WITH THE OWNER'S PERMISSION
THIS BOTHY IS MAINTAINED
BY
THE MOUNTAIN BOTHY ASSOCIATION.

Beneath this declaration in red italic lettering was the clear instruction.

Please keep the place tidy

Doc pushed the door; it creaked loudly, almost comically as we stepped into the small porch. An interior door opened into a short hallway, fixed on the wall was a map of the area and an old framed picture. The image was of the last permanent inhabitants. A dour-looking wee man and his equally cheerless wife stared morosely from a fading sepia image. Even their stocky little ponies looked totally pissed off. In another age, before the advent of the Land Rover and ATV, they had lived here and attended to the land when it belonged to a Victorian sporting estate.

Ignoring the doors ahead and to the right, Doc opened the door to the left and stepped into the silent empty room. The only furnishings two metal chairs with cracked plastic seats. Three of the walls were panelled, with smoke-stained pine the fourth, rough hewn stone with a built-in fireplace into which a wood-burning stove was set. The sill of the deeply recessed window was covered in a sheet of tin, stained with grease and a kaleidoscopic array of candle waxes. This served as the kitchen.

We staggered eagerly across the wooden floor, ingrained with dirt and worn smooth from a thousand muddy boots then flopped onto a knee-high platform set along one wall. Easing the packs off our aching shoulders, we lay there and groaned loudly in ecstatic relief. Doc was first to rouse as he pulled plastic bags full of food from his pack and hung them on the myriad nails and cup hooks that dotted the graffiti ridden wall around the window. These hooks were vital; food left on the floor belonged to the numerous hungry Bothy mice.

Doc quickly set up his 'WhisperLite' stove on the recessed windowsill and lit the burner. It reverberated with a throaty roar, a welcome focal point of heat and light in the cold empty room.

"Tea?" he barked.

"Pardon?" I yelled to compete with the roaring flame of the ironically-named stove.

"Aye very fuckin' funny, do you want tea or do you no'?"

"Here how many years is that you've been lugging that piece of crap around for?"

"Fer fucksake, Scully, just cause you always buy the latest whizz bang shit, this piece of kit is tried and tested!"

"Aye, well here," I cheerfully slammed down my cup and headed along the short corridor, my footstep echoed as I shouted, "Maybe Heidi's in the other room; I'll go check!"

I opened the door and a rather strange sight greeted me: Someone had converted a bench, and now nailed to it at a rigid right angle, like a church pew, was a rough rectangular frame.

"Oh hey Doc, get in here, c'mon give us a hand with this!"

Doc stomped down the short corridor, "Yah beauty," he exclaimed, and after a close examination of the furniture added, "Aye, would say it's a Chippendale, probably late seventies, and judging by the quality of the woodwork, most likely built by a one-armed blind plumber. Now tell me madam, has it been in yer family long?"

"Aye, it's an heirloom, yah comedian, now c'mon give us a hand."

With that, we took an end each and half dragged, half carried the crudely constructed bench along the short corridor. We swapped it for the cracked plastic and metal chairs and placed it facing the unlit fire then cautiously tested the comfort level.

"Hang on," I jumped up and returned moments later with a dirty-looking synthetic sleeping bag; its last occupant had apparently been a muddy wet dog. "Was in the other room. *Now…*" proudly, I draped the grubby sleeping bag over the bench and strapped it into place with a bungee cord, "It's a Chesterfield!"

Sitting down again, we exclaimed in mutual delight.

"Soft yet rather smelly furnishing this year, what a luxury!"

"Aye, fuckin' luxury!"

A steady plume of steam belched from the kettle and condensed onto the cold glass of the window, I grabbed the Bothy guest book and we dragged the chairs outside. Sat in the lee of the porch in the ebbing light of the day, we sipped piping hot tea and smoked cigarettes.

"Well that wasnae too bad," I lied, as muscles not used in years fired off regular notes of complaint.

"Aye, it was a doddle; mind you, I have to say I was a wee bit worried by how totally fucked I felt when we reached the top of the first hill," Doc whipped out his hip flask, "Painkiller?" he asked and without waiting for an answer deftly streamed a generous shot of golden whisky into his tea then mine.

"*Ta*, and aye true, I was knackered after lifting my pack out the van when it was only half full; still, we soon got our second wind!"

"Aye, just enough left in ma' tank for the slog through the bog."

I shuddered at the painful memory, placed my cup on a convenient rock and picked up the Bothy guestbook to flip through the thumb-smudged pages. Each one revealed snippets of its history, scrawled in a rainbow of inky threads tying together the tales of privation and the extremes of weather or alcohol consumption reported by the many guests who had sought the shelter of its crooked slate roof.

"Oh, here it says the MBA boys came in at New Year, they did some repairs, took away a few bags of rubbish and made the Chippendale."

"Aye fuck, well, I think they'll like what we've done ti it!"

"Here, check it out," I held the book open at an entry from many years ago.

Doc frowned and peered myopically at the inscription, "Aye, now that was a while back, long time, a long, long time!"

"That one was a great weekend though, here, that was when Banjo brought whisky wrapped in his spare clothes, but left it in the bottle. I can still see the look on his face when he dropped the pack and heard the sound of breaking glass!"

"Oh aye, ho ho, he used a plastic bag so that held the whisky right? Eh he had ti strain it through a pair of boxers, to get rid of the glass did he no'?"

"Aye indeed, White Horse Whisky we promptly re-named it 'Wet Arse Whisky' as I recall and he wore said boxers on the outside of his pants for the rest of the weekend. Oh and look! The inscription written by the man himself!" I laughed happily, "Now that was some weekend!"

"Aye, they *all* fuckin' were!"

I stared at the scrawled spidery writing for a moment. A vision of Banjo hunched over the book, pen in hand, flitted briefly through my mind as I snapped the book shut and swapped it for my cup of tea. Doc had darted into the Bothy, and when he returned he handed me a plastic bag containing a small brass plaque and six nails.

"Oh, good job, good job," a lump formed in my throat as I read the engraving. "Take it we're waiting till we're all here before we put it up?"

"Aye 'course!"

As I silently re-read the inscription, a rapidly setting winter sun shone through broken clouds as they drifted over the horizon. The light glinted weakly off Loch Ericht as a gentle wind drifted from Ben Alder's icy flank and brought a hint of even more Arctic air. It rippled the dead stalks of reedy grass by the lochside, and found the patch of cold sweat on my back. I shivered, "Better go get wood then, eh?"

"Aye, fuck s'pose."

We crossed the bridge on aching limbs and climbed slowly back along the route we had taken only half an hour earlier. The massive bulk of Ben Alder towered over the Bothy its snow cover solid from the bealach, a high pass, to the summit. Temporarily cleared of cloud the summit peak gleamed pristine and white, its rough contours smoothed by the coating of snow like frosting on confectionary.

Northwards at the top of the glen sat the imposing bulk of Aonach Beag, a ridge running west to east joined it to Carn Dearg; in contrast to their white tops the sky looked dark, almost purple, ominous and heavy with either rain or snow. A steadily building wind moved it our way.

"Here, Donald and Robbie should be tramping down there someplace," I pointed at the winding path snaking for four rough and undulating miles to the head of the glen.

"Aye, well that's assuming they've no' been waylaid by alcohol."

I laughed at that, as ever Doc the master of unintentional irony.

Having taken the train, the others would have approached by trekking the thirteen miles from the isolated station at Corrour. They would have watched as the train rumbled off and rapidly dwindled to leave them stood in the middle of nowhere. The only building for miles around the Corrour Station Hotel and Restaurant accessible only by rail would have been dark and silent, shut for the winter season.

Doc had told me that Robbie had actually been less than enthusiastic when it was suggested he traveled in with Donald. He had indicated that it would have been more entertaining for him to travel with us than with our more stoic companion, but the logic was undeniable. Travelling in pairs was always safer; ankles could twist, and a slip could result in a deadly fall into an ice-cold river. In these parts at this time of year you could wait for days until someone trekked the same path.

It took us some time, but eventually we located an old pine tree downed by a winter storm. Its shallow root system had stuck incongruously into the cold air with a stubborn death grip on the peaty soil, and rocks that had once held it upright. We worked quickly, built up a large pile of wood, split it into four bundles and returned to the Bothy with two of them. I splashed across the shallow stream then dropped my pile of wood by the front door with an expletive-laden grunt. Doc followed moments later but slipped and sat briefly in the ice-cold water. As he stomped into the Bothy and pulled off his wet leggings he yelled, "Fuck! Fell on my arse in the fuckin' river!"

I looked around in the fading light as a dripping Doc bared his wee white arse and rummaged for dry clothes.

"Eh, kettle's on," was my consoling reply as I turned to hide a half suppressed grin, then added, "still no sign of Heidi, though!"

3 NO SIGNAL

Dried off with the chill warmed by another whisky-laced tea we headed out and started on the woodpile.

"Here, did you see that?" Doc had paused squinting into the black sky.

"Aye might have been." I peered round the corner of the Bothy, the flash of a head torch appeared, it bobbed and weaved through the darkness.

"Ho!" Doc waved a hand slowly across the light of his head torch.

"Ho!" came a distant reply with an accompanying single slow flash.

"I'll get the kettle on, put a wee nip in their tea" Doc announced.

He returned a few moments later to find Robbie had me enveloped in a bear hug embrace.

"Fer fuck sake!" he'd grumbled, as Robbie turned and cheerfully hugged him, "You're like a Gore-Tex clad puppy dog! Are you going ti lick my face now?"

"Aye, if you'd like," Robbie grinned, his cheeks flush from exercise, excitement and no doubt relief at having reached the Bothy.

"Acht fuck off, here, how was the hike?"

"Aye easy peasy lemon squeezy, you?"

"Aye, a doddle, now where's Doughboy?"

"No' far back, he'll be here soon enough!" Robbie turned and examined the dark building, the light from his head torch flickered across the granite façade. "So, THIS is the famous haunted Bothy then?"

"Aye, chock full of *evil* spirits, all eighteen years old, wet an' peaty brown!" Doc grinned at his own joke

Chuckling, Robbie headed into the Bothy and effortlessly eased an oversized pack off his broad shoulders and onto the bench with a satisfied groan. His physique, and his outfit of camouflage jacket, pea green waterproof pants and heavy black leather boots, all residual benefits of his time in the Army. His current employment as a park ranger and general handyman was a physical outdoor lifestyle he loved. In addition, the free accommodation was an added perk shared with his wife and young son.

I followed him in, "here how's your folks, Robbie, they doin' alright?"

"Aye they're good, an' yours?" Sweaty steam billowed out as he unzipped his jacket.

"Aye, spoke to them but I've no' seen 'em, came straight from the airport, I'll catch up next week. How's Sarah and wee Colin? Here, has she let you back out yet since yer night out with Doc?"

As he grinned, his face lit up, "Oh, now *that* was a good night!"

Doc fiddled with the whisperlight, "here kettle's on, did you remember ti bring a cup?"

"Aye, here you go one cup," Robbie pulled off his hat and vigorously rubbed his blond hair, flattened and soaked with sweat.

I could sense Doc's irritation as Robbie used his lofty frame to easily reach over and place the cup on the shelf. He scowled darkly, fiddled with the stove and muttered, "It's getting dark in the land of the giants!"

"Better put a candle in the window then, yah midget!" Robbie grinned cheekily.

"Fuck off!" was the curt and predictable response.

"Aye indeed, Robbie. "I chimed in cheerfully, "Just as the song says. Tell you what, we slogged in here once a night walk and it clouded over. Went as black as the Earl of Hell's waistcoat and then started pelting us with rain and sleet. Me n' Doc here were thrashing about falling in bogs totally, totally exhausted *and* way off course."

"Aye, except Scully here was sure he knew where he was!"

"Tsk, whatever. Anyway, we topped the ridge over there. Donald and Banjo had walked in earlier eh, we could see the candle." I paused, lit another small candle and placed it on the window ledge, "Led us out of the darkness to safety. Tell you though, talk about ecstasy, I think I might even have kissed Doc."

"Aye, right, I'd have kicked you in yer fat nuts if you'd tried."

As we stood and sipped whisky-laced tea in the candlelit semi-darkness, Donald's silhouette flitted past the window, then in he strode to an enthusiastic welcome.

"Alright now, lads, we all made it then?"

His voice was soft and lilting in a Highland accent acquired during a youth misspent on the Black Isle near Inverness. The many years of helping out on his father's farm had given him a tough muscular core, and a frigid East Coast wind had bestowed a thick skin. When the farm went bust, he had moved South to a more sedentary lifestyle, but retained his dietary habits and turned many a muscle into flab. For this hike he had worn a black ushanka, a Soviet-era winter hat with the earflaps tied up, and his faded orange jacket, which he still favoured even though Doc insisted on referring to its shade of colour as 'old man's piss'.

Scuffed and worn waterproof pants and a threadbare fleece top over a thermal t-shirt completed his outfit. His unkempt appearance was aided and abetted by slightly bloodshot brown eyes and scrubby ginger stubble, a consequence of both the eleven-mile hike from Corrour and an uncomfortable night spent on a sofa in his older sister's front room in Glasgow. This had all been compounded by a few late drinks on the Dumbarton Road. At the eleventh hour, he had chosen the sofa and drinking over trying to get over from the Isle of Arran to make the early Queen Street rendezvous with Robbie and their train. These days, the island was his home, its picturesque distillery his current place of employment.

Pushing us aside, he dropped his pack with a groan.

"So, what the fuck kept you then?"

"Ocht, fit bastard, *and* I put an extra four cans of Eccy in his pack, to slow him down." He chuckled removed the ushanka, vigorously rubbing his face.

"Eh, you did *what!*" Robbie's shocked look was in sharp contrast to our delighted faces, "When the fuck did you do that?"

"Well, it was when you went off to rid yourself of that Scotrail coffee," Donald winked slyly at me as he relayed the tale, "he disappears for a quick dump so I added the cans to his pack. He was awfully proud of himself as well, so he was; told me he felt about five pounds lighter!"

"Just as well, eh, that's about the weight of they cans?"

"Ocht aye, well, we had stopped to hide the bag for our return journey."

"What, our shoes and the eight cans of Eccy?" Robbie was still pouting.

"Well aye, but there's only four now; still it didn't work did it, yah young pup? You still got here well 'afore me! Anyway, I see there's plenty of wood."

"Aye, we cut four bundles but only carried two back, so it's ready for the morn, just needs to be retrieved."

"Excellent, excellent," Donald produced a hip flask, "Ocht here, now that calls for a wee celebration libation I would say. Eh... but first tell me lads, what is *that?*" He gestured curtly at the roughly-made bench, draped in its dirty sleeping bag.

"Tsk, it's a Chesterfield, isn't that obvious?"

"It was a fuckin Chippendale when we got here!"

"Ocht of course it is, silly me!" he scowled and sat down. I suppressed a grin as the Chesterfield creaked slightly under his chubby arse. "Ocht, now boys, *this* is luxury!"

Donald nodded approvingly as a broad smile crinkled his bulbous nose and almost hid his eyes.

The room filled rapidly with the warmth and happy chatter of old friends meeting again. More domestic and work-related questions were asked and answered and a hip flask emptied, then we headed out into the darkness to finish sawing wood. We soon had the wet logs packed around the woodstove, tapered up towards the chimney.

Donald fished a box of firelighters from his pack and got the fire going, then he stood slowly and groaned at his aches and pains. "Here now, is this it Doc?" A set of reading glasses were produced as he pulled the brass plaque from its bag.

"Aye 'tis we'll wait for daylight an' find a good spot."

"Probably the porch or by the front door?" Robbie was also reading the inscription by the light of his head torch. "That looks great Doc, really good job; it's perfect, really fitting."

Doc just took a swig of whisky and added, "aye, fuck it, yer due me five quid each."

Robbie rummaged in his pack and pulled out the extra beer cans, as he did he grumbled, "Cheeky wee fucker," in Donald's direction.

"Ocht well it didn't slow you down, much!"

"Wee shite," he mumbled as he retrieved his phone.

"Fer fuck sake Robbie!"

Robbie froze, phone clutched in his hand his guilt illuminated by the beam of Doc's head torch.

"Aye told you what was here," growled at the sight of the phone then tapped his head torch, "This is for light, the shovels for yer shite and no, you'll no' get a *signal!*"

"Aye well, I thought I'd check."

"Aye here, I had two bars on the top of Aonach Beag one year," I casually informed them from my seat next to the growing fire. "Of course the wind was howling like a total fuckin' banshee and it was minus ridiculous. So, I certainly wasnae taking my gloves off and standing about trying to order pizza!"

"Aye well you *might* get reception from the top of Beinn Bheoil, *if* it was an *emergency*." Doc scowled darkly at the phone as Robbie quickly shoved it in his pocket.

"Ocht here now," Donald smiled, "Robbie, if they really need us they know where we are and if you want the current news for these parts, well check the Bothy book!"

"Aye, we looked, hasnae been anyone here since New Year when the MBA boys came in by boat and cleaned up a bit…" I slapped the padded bench and cheerfully added, "And they brought the Chippendale."

"Aye well, there you go," Doc scanned the room, "no one else but us daft enough ti try an' get in at this time of year!"

4 SHIT-EATING GRIN

Above the fireplace, wet socks, sweaty t-shirts and other items had been draped across the drying rack, and one by one our boots were lined up in a neat row close to the fire. As he inspected his socks and massaged his toes, Robbie asked, "Here now, anyone getting hungry?".

Donald responded with a howl of delighted laughter followed by, "Ocht, I knew it!"

"Knew what?"

"That you'd be first to mention food!"

"Ah get ti fuck, right let's get this party started, pasta methinks!"

"Aye go on yerself young Robbie," My stomach had reverted to it usual Ben Alder mode of permanent gnawing hunger.

Donald held up a hand, "ocht now hold on before you start pigging out, let us take stock. Now, how much scran and bevvy have we got?"

"Eh, let me see," Doc grabbed bags from around the window and swiftly emptied the contents onto the bench. We gathered around and followed suit, quickly generating a large pile of Super Noodles, Smash, pasta, cheese, peanuts, mini Mars bars, bacon, pitta breads, eggs, sausages, tea bags and powdered milk. .

"Here, now what's this?" I held up a mysterious bag and inspected the contents in the dim light.

"Oh aye that, is a quarter pound of trail mix!"

"Oh without any added Peruvian marching dust I trust?"

"Acht fuck," Doc shook his head wryly, pursed his lips and affected a comical look of deep sadness.

"Peruvian marching dust?" Do explain.

"Aye, see Robbie, good few years back Banjo had a party and someone left behind a little bag of a coke and speed. Anyway, we were headed to the Pentlands for a wee hike so it went into the trail mix. Now, he vehemently maintained it wouldnae have had that much effect on a mouse, but somehow under some sort of psychosomatic influence, we crisscrossed the hills in record time. Then straight to the Alan Ramsey for a pint…"

"Here that's my local pub these days!"

"Aye Robbie, grand boozer right enough our problem was none of us could move for the next few days due to some pretty excruciatingly painful muscles, so, we never did add Peruvian marching dust to our trail mix again."

"Aye nae kidding!"

"Ocht aye, he was some boy was Banjo!"

"Talking of which who brought whisky in a *glass* bottle, was that lesson no' learnt?" Doc pointed accusingly at the offending item on the shelf.

"Aye that was me but I'd wrapped in bubble wrap and double bagged it, I'd run out of plastic!" Robbie explained defensively.

"Aye Asda Malt, wouldnae want such quality whisky staining yer clothes, Robbie!"

Ignoring the sarcasm Robbie continued, "Well, I also brought this eh… for emergencies," he produced a small plastic pouch with a black cap.

"What is *this*?" Doc snatched the pouch and frowned darkly at the label. "Robbie what, in the name of fuck, is Optimum Blended Whisky?"

"I picked it up in Tesco's its no' glass so, safer," he grinned proudly.

"Aye" after twisting off the black top, Doc took a tentative sip, his face contorted in disgust. "Ohh that is boggin' seriously, it's like paint stripper."

"Ocht now how would you know what paint stripper taste like Doc?"

"Fuck, you want?" The pouch was thrust at Donald.

"Ocht now Robbie that *is* rank; I've tasted better Pocheen."

Donald offered the pouch to me; I sipped and promptly gagged at the foul taste. "Here, Tonto's brought the firewater! Robbie, what the fuck are you doing to us, man? That is truly awful!"

"Well like I said *it is* for emergencies!" Robbie's youthful face had crumpled into a crestfallen look, "Now here I also brought a nice Jamaica Cake and…"

"Jamaica Cake?"

"No, he bought it."

"Fuck off, Scully that is shite, yer puns are pure piss!"

"And I brought this!" slowly, and to spontaneous applause, Robbie pulled an eighteen-inch-long Stornaway Black Pudding blood sausage from his pack and hung it proudly on the wall.

"Ocht, I think we have adequate provisions, we *should* just about scrape through the three nights."

"Time ti eat some of it then!" I declared, my comment was met with a unanimous, 'aye'

We crowded around the small cooking space like hungry dogs around a food bowl, politely jostling each other with not so subtle nudges, driven by the voracious appetite a day hiking in the fresh air generates.

The windowsill was soon a cluttered mass of stoves and bubbling pots, packets of pasta and Super Noodles were thrown in with scant regard for cooking instructions.

A brief time later we were crouched over our plates sat round the fire, and through clouds of steam illuminated by our head torch beams we each ceremoniously opened a can of McEwans Export.

"Slainte!" the Celtic toast reverberated around the room, followed by a contented silence broken only by the rapid scrape of plastic forks on plastic plates and the occasional appreciative resonate belch. Empty plates soon clattered noisily onto the windowsill as the kettle boiled and the whisky circulated once more. As head torches were switched off one by one, the room fell dark and the light cast by the flickering fire projected four dancing shadows onto the wood-paneled wall like a Bothy Bunruka.

"Ocht, now that filled a gap; now more tea anyone?"

"Oh aye!"

"Oh aye and put a nip in mine will yah Doughboy?" Doc kicked on his boots, "I think it's my turn ti get water and there's the dishes to do!"

"I'll give you a hand," I jumped to my feet, "Here Doc, did I ever tell you the one about the bishop, the hooker, and the camel?" For some reason, the mention of getting water brought to mind this joke.

"Aww ti fuck," he exhaled in a weary sigh.

"Well…" I began as Doc slammed the outside door behind us.

When we returned, I dropped the icy wet plates on the shelf, crouched shivering by the fire and grumbled, "fuck it is Baltic out there!"

"Ocht here, now put a dram in it." Donald suggested as he handed me a cup of tea. The corner of a tea bag broke through the surface like a shark's dorsal fin and cruised in a slow, lazy circle through little lumpy icebergs of unmixed powdered milk. I plucked it out and flicked it deftly into the fire; it lay there, hissed then started to burn.

"Here what was the joke then?"

"*Don't,* Scully it wasnae funny first time!"

"Aye well, now Scully tell me, do you reckon you've settled in the old US of A?"

"Well in the Northeast, aye," I replied cautiously, I knew Donald had a view of the US that tended towards liking it to the Great Satan. "Beantown is the business; great place, I really like it!"

He frowned thoughtfully, "Really, so you've no plans to return then?"

Before I could answer Robbie butted in with his usual youthful enthusiasm, "hey Scully you'll come home to an independent Scotland though, aye?"

"Well maybe if there's a job for me or I'll come back for my holidays and drop a few greenbacks on you."

"It's going to be great," Robbie enthused, "independence, we'll be our own masters; none of this kowtowing to Westminster!"

I had no time to respond to this before Doc let out a loud and derisive snort, "Aye, that'll be fuckin' right, Robbie: politicians, lying bastards the whole lot of them, they just tell you what you want ti hear, most would sell their own grannies to get into power!"

"Aw c'mon Doc," Robbie protested weakly as he struggled to think of an appropriate counter to the scathing appraisal.

"Ocht well Doc, at least there would be some accountability they'll not be four hundred miles away in their ivory towers. But here, we're getting off-topic," Donald turned back to me and studied my face in the dim light. "So, Scully, do you not miss Edinburgh or Scotland then?"

"Aye of course I do; I mean, I do like Boston, though it has to be said the locals really arenie that friendly and they seriously cannae drive for shit!"

"That'll explain why you're no' missing Embra' then. Sounds like a home fi home." Doc got in his usual dig at Edinburgh's reputation for less than convivial behavior. I had the perfect response.

"Ah fuck off, yah soap dodger, we all know they had to call it Glasgow because sphincter was already taken!"

"Fuck off!" he laughed, stung by the retort but delighted by the humor.

"Aye well you know I've had some cracking nights out in Boston and some pretty good and memorable times in the States in general. *But...* I reckon most, all even, are nothing compared to some of the capers we all got up to!"

"Aye, fer sure."

"Question is, is that me missing Scotland or me missing my youth?"

"I'm no' missing mine, I'm still having it, yeah maudlin old fart."

"Ah, fuck off yah young pup, anyway you know what it is weird, the stuff you really do miss. A decent bacon roll made with back bacon, no' that streaky shite. No' having to explain some of your perceived eccentricities, or walking the timeless streets of Edinburgh's old town. These days when I'm back, I actually notice the architecture! Of course, there's always getting out on the winter hills, or when the mountains are purple or green in their summer regalia."

"Fuckin' *regalia*, Scully, you an' yer fancy words! Can you no' speak normal, man?"

I smiled serenely, ignored Doc and continued to expound, "But hey, work life, all that shit, long since got in the way It's no' as if I'd be guaranteed getting away any more than once a year even if I lived here!"

"Ocht aye, well, living in Scotland is in my opinion the way to go, but regardless at least we can all still contemplate doing this!" Donald swept his arm to indicate the Bothy. "Ocht I mean, when you consider the scrapes and the capers we got up to." The laughter that followed this analysis grew louder as he glanced slyly at Doc and added, "And yet somehow we all managed to stay out of jail!"

"Hope yer no' referring ti me, Doughboy!"

"Aye I was, you car thief!"

"You got in it yah fuckin hippy crit."

"Whey wha… what's this all about then?"

"Well see Robbie," I stifled a laugh at Doc's clever play on words and his oblique reference to our more hirsute past. "We once got back home from Glastonbury with no money by borrowing a motor from a couple of lads…"

"Aye they deserved it," Doc quickly cut me off keen to give his own version of the events. "See Robbie, they thought we were burdz on account of the long hair we had back then. Stopped to pick us up and when they realized we had the meat and two veg, they threw a can of beer over me!"

"*You* had long hair?"

"Ocht aye but you could still see his ears!"

"Fuck off, yah wee fat shite!"

"Ho steady," I held out my hands and took on the role of peacemaker. "Aye, so see we caught up with them after walking for what felt like hours, they'd gone into a pub, so Doc here nicked their car and drove us home."

"Well that seems a bit much just for soaking you with beer Doc, but aye needs must I suppose and they'd have got it back?"

"Aye probably he only damaged the steering column a wee bit but you know what Robbie I bet they were no' best pleased when they found out Banjo had taken a shit under the spare tire."

"YAH WHAT!"

"Aye well c'mon Scully we were all a bit younger and wilder then. Cannae stay daft wee laddies for ever now can we?"

I quickly grabbed my own nose with one hand and used the other to vibrate my chin as I began singing in a highly nasal warbling style the first few lines from 'Forever Young' by Bob Dylan.

Doc just reached for the whisky and dryly noted. "Aye well we're no' all here though are we, well no' in body at least!"

"Aye," A collective sigh reverberated as the mood became somber.

"Ocht now, he was some boy, sorely missed, always with that big shit-eating grin on his face."

I had a silent chuckle at that comment. I strongly suspected that Donald, who had frequently been the brunt of Banjo's practical jokes, had always been just a little jealous of that big shit-eating grin. Whatever you wanted to call it, when Banjo was in the company, well, the girls seemed to play a little more with their hair and laugh a little louder at his jokes. If it wasn't that grin, well, maybe that head of curly black hair flopping down over his deep brown eyes and that perpetually youthful face. He had the kind of looks that meant even other guys knew he was handsome. A modern-day Robert Burns, and the more than passing resemblance wasn't the only thing he had in common with the 18th century poet. Burns had once written 'Sweetest hours that ever I spend are spent amongst the lasses O...' Aye that had been Banjo right enough, a ladies man.

"Feels though we eh, should have an empty seat by the fire, in absentia, after all didn't Banjo always refer to this Bothy as our 'Hotel Caledonia'!"

"Ocht aye, you can check out anytime but you can never leave..." Donald mumbled softly lest Robbie had failed to grasp the inference.

"Fuck *that*," roared Doc, "it's way too cold and here one thing I know! He'd no' have wanted a big fuss but fer sure he'd be happy that we'd all came back to the Bothy wi' the usual weekend of hills and whisky planned. And one more thing, if was any of us, he'd be sat right *there*, shit-eating grin an' all, knocking back a dram an' telling stories about each of you!"

"Aye now that's very true, very, very true."

Doc had hit the nail on the head. Yes, we came here to scatter ashes but that was only one part of the catharsis, although we may have heard these stories before it would not stop us fondly recollecting and telling them all over again. Maybe even adding a few embellishments as the whisky flowed readily by the light of the crackling fire.

"Well we all made it through the hassles of winter travel so now all we need is good weather the morn or at least no so bad that we cannae reach the fuckin' summit!" Doc nodded at the window, the wind had picked up and now it rattled the glass and eagerly searched the old pine panels for cracks and gaps.

"Aye surely that's no' too much to ask?" Robbie looked hopefully around the room.

There was no reply we all just stared in thoughtful silence at the fire.

5 MANATEES DO NOT WEAR MIRROR SHADES

Robbie had been holding a can of beer upside down, his head tilted back as he ensured he got every last drop. Satisfied, he reached for his knife that hung in a sheath on his belt, but he did this a little too quickly. Responding to the distinctive sound, Doc tensed, so imperceptibly it was barely noticed. Robbie certainly did not, but I did. Casually I thrust out a whisky bottle and provided a barrier between them. I need not have worried. Doc relaxed. It was a knee jerk, some old almost forgotten Pavlovian reflex from an earlier period of his life.

Carefully, Robbie proceeded to slit the can lengthways, turned it around and cut across the top and bottom then peeled it open. Satisfied with his work, he impaled the can on a nail that stuck from the chimney and placed a tea light candle in the bottom. The added illumination offered by the reflective surface of the inside of the can was minimal to say the least.

Ignoring Robbie, who appeared to be waiting for applause or recognition Donald instead turned to me. "So here, you still riding your mountain bike?"

"Aye no' as much on an actual mountain though, mainly into work 'n back, less need for the spandex lederhosen with an inbuilt chapatti to stop chaffing the fuck out my isnie?"

"Eh, your isnie?" Robbie frowned quizzically.

"The bit in-between," explained Doc patiently, "isnie yer arsehole isnie yer baws."

"Aye, ha-ha, nice," Robbie chuckled.

"Here now," I sat up a little straighter and smiled happily as I recollected, "remember the time we cycled up Glen Glass and Banjo took a header?"

"Ocht aye," Donald cried, "I was sure that was going to need stitches!"

"That's how he got the scar over his eye, Robbie."

"Oh really, he once told me he came off a mountain bike, nothing more."

"Aye well, see, this was a few years back now," Donald paused and nodded to indicate myself and Doc, "we, had decided to head out to climb Stob Goer one Sunday, and we took bikes in case the hill was out. True to form it was pissing down so we decided instead to go up Glen Glass. Now see, after about two miles, the rain eased off and then pretty much stopped, so we all shed some gear and kept going. Of course, the sun only goes and comes out and by the time we reach the first lochan it was actually getting pretty warm, at least in the glen."

"Aye you're right there Donald, it was sweaty work!"

"Well now, we eventually stopped found a wee sandy cove with a soft bank of heather and had lunch. By this time we're in t-shirts; gorgeous spot too, stunning view, lochan trout poking up their noses all over. Now, course as we're on the bikes, Scully here had thoughtfully packed a few beers! So by the time we set off we had quite a buzz on 'course Banjo only jumps on his bike and shouts 'last one back is a fuckin' numpty or similar.' So off we went, it was mad racing mountain bikes when you've had a few!"

"Aye, I couldnae have kept up with Banjo if I'd been sober, he was flying BUT the inevitable happened and we come round a bend to find he'd turned himself into a Centaur-cycle which is of course what the ancient Greeks would have called a half man half mountain bike!"

"Aye fer fuck he was a bit of a mess right enough, it was hard to tell exactly where the bike stopped and Banjo began!"

"Ocht aye, but here this was Banjo, so of course he was still grinning, even though there was blood all over his face, I was actually planning to put a couple of stitches in it, but a few minutes with a compress did the job."

"Aye but his bike was fucked, front forks bent wheel all twisted, so nowt for it but to walk!" Doc scowled as he recalled the struggle, "Banjo ended up trying to carry his then we tried strapping two bikes together but the path was too narrow so it became a bit of a slog!"

"Couldnae leave him to it of course Robbie no' with a head wound!"

"Now then," Donald held up a hand, eager to regain his mantle of chief storyteller, "there was an upside, see after a few miles the river formed a very, very inviting looking pool. We were sweating buckets by then so, that was it, I jumped in, followed in double quick time by Scully, Doc then, Banjo. You know what Robbie, in no time at all it became vaguely reminiscent of a family holiday in Florida." Donald paused and waited for Robbie to respond.

"Florida, what? It wasnae *that* warm, was it?"

"Ocht no, not the water temperature, no it was more the wildlife, but see, Robbie, the difference was that in Florida... the Manatees *do not* wear mirror shades!"

Donald rode contentedly on the wave of delighted laughter his chubby cheeks catching the glow of the firelight.

Robbie chuckled gleefully and noted, "Aye, yards of pale white Scottish flesh finally being exposed to the sun after a long winter then?

Nodding vigorously, clearly pleased that he had grasped his pictorial euphemism, Donald continued. "Ocht well, the water was a pretty refreshing temperature to say the least so I'd soon had enough even with my tough Highland blood."

"Is that what they call flab in Inverness?"

"Feck off! Now… you know Robbie I was drying myself with a pair of socks when I learnt two things, actually no, three of varying degrees of value."

"Aye?" I smiled, Donald was on a roll and who knew what he might come out with next.

"Well the first, was I *do* like the feel of wool on my he-haws!"

"Aye right, like you didnae ken that already, yah sheep shagger!"

"Ocht yes, now, the second was that Scully here can easily hide his dick in four inches of peaty water."

"Oi. fuck off Doughboy that water was cold!"

"Yes aha and the third was that Doc here has a very, very hairy arse!" Donald turned and addressed Doc; he questioned him with a practiced look of innocence, his face cherubic. "Here, Doc could you not, ah, grow it long and comb it up over yer big baldy head?"

"Fuck off! Yah wee fat bastard!" Doc laughed as he plucked a plastic bottle from the shelf. "Here have we run out of whisky, or is it just me?" Cup in one hand, bottle in the other, he poured whisky into the various beverage containers offered for replenishment.

Robbie stood and pushed his feet into his boots.

"Aye, time for me to shake the snake an' all," I reached for my boots.

"Aye right wiggle the worm you mean!"

We shrugged on our jackets and stepped out into the frigid night air and howling wind. Stood in the lee of the building we watched as the wind whipped the snow. The flakes blurred in the beams of light from our head torches like we were standing as a massive meteor shower rushed past.

"Jeez," I shivered, "Glad we're no' walking in in this!"

"Aye, brutal!" Robbie agreed, "Here, how come all those years ago Banjo didnae say, 'lets go someplace warm 'n sunny'!"

"Beer bravado, Robbie, he had the idea in a pub; funny thing was in the cold light of dawn it still seemed like a great idea! Well, to a select few at least!"

"Well, it was a cracking walk, some great views, and now it's got warm and toasty with the whisky flowing, so I'm sold."

Instinctively, Robbie reached into his pocket and pulled out his phone. He paused and shivered as the screen slowly came to life, but there was no signal, so no text to check, and no missing calls.

"Fer fuck sake Robbie can you no' leave the outside world alone?"

"Aye sorry, habit I guess," embarrassed, he quickly replaced the phone and followed me back to the warmth of the Bothy. As we passed the window of the empty room, the beams of light from our head torches played across the floor and the cold stone fireplace.

Suddenly, a soft but sudden noise behind us startled Robbie and he turned. The searchlight beam from his torch seared the darkness. Several pairs of eerily bright unblinking eyes reflected back.

"Fer fuck," he gasped, as both hands clutched for the cold stone of the Bothy.

Then a soft snort was followed by several heavy dull thuds, hooves hitting frozen ground, as the stag and its harem rose from the heather and moved further from the shelter of the Bothy into the night. Robbie laughed in nervous relief and shivering from the chill tried to push past me as we clattered through the door.

"Fuck…" he announced as he squeezed onto the bench and held his palms outstretched towards the fire.

"What's up?"

"Robbie here just got spooked by Bambi's dad."

"Aye, but you know just before that I was looking into the window of the empty room, and I dunno," Robbie's eyes opened wide as he stared at the fire, "Well, it was like someone stepped on my grave."

"Ocht… Has the other room got the hairs goin' on the back of yer neck then?"

Robbie said nothing, but nodded as his teeth chattered slightly.

"Here ever noticed how warm places arenie spooky?" I winked at Doc, who of course sneered at my comment, but I knew even he found the setting transcendental, not that he would ever use such a word. There was just something about the setting of the Bothy in winter that could send an involuntary shiver down any spine. This, our silent dark granite sanctuary from the harsh winter storms.

"Ocht aye, all these years coming here and the place can still give me the willies; still that's what the whisky's for!"

Donald cheerfully poured a large dram into Robbie's tea. He was right of course we would chase away the silence and the cold with light, heat, whisky and of course, a lot of laughter.

Donald switched the topic abruptly it seemed to take Robbie off guard. "Ocht now then, you been out recently, taken Sarah to see any good bands?"

"Ah no not really, no' had the chance," he hesitated, and took a quick swig from his cup and swiftly changed the subject. "So eh… is Mhari still liking it on Arran?"

"Ocht fine, think she likes it there, pretty laid back, suits her and the boys, that's four years since we moved onto the island; we've been married almost twenty!" Donald smiled proudly at the mention of this achievement.

"Here Doughboy, if you'd just have stabbed her instead of wedding her you'd be out of jail by now on good behavior."

Doc's blurted comment silenced Donald instantly. A look of anger flashed across his rapidly reddening face and he clenched his fists. Oblivious or just indifferent to Donald's irate expression Doc continued, his cup held aloft like a master of ceremonies. "Here's ti marriage a-k-a, time served and to keeping the right arm injury free thereby at least guaranteeing a regular sex life! You know, you start bickering about the littlest things, like the argument we had before I left about the marmalade!"

"Eh…?"

"Well it wasnae about marmalade exactly, what happened was I meant ti ask her ti pass the marmalade and it just came out all wrong."

I had to smirk as Robbie, all wide-eyed and innocent turned to Doc and demanded, "How can pass the marmalade come out all wrong?"

"Well see that's what I meant… I meant to say pass the marmalade but instead it came out as, 'You fuckin' bitch you've ruined my life!'"

As Robbie stared, mouth open eyes wide, I again filled the void with a roar of laughter and almost splattered a mouthful of my whisky-laden tea across the floor.

Warming to his caustic diatribe, Doc continued. "Aye, these days we are just two complete fuckin' strangers. Well, actually hold the fuckin' part that's gone along wi' the lobster thermidor."

"You know… ah think this is all getting a wee bit cynical it *cannae* be that bad, Doc!" I searched his face for a response; he did not return my gaze. The feeling of apprehension grew; marriage was perhaps not a topic we should discuss. Doc might just blurt out what he had seen in the Tass, not an ideal way for Robbie to learn about Sara's supposed infidelity.

Finally, Doc slowly raised his cup and in a bitter voice toasted, "Inertia!"

"Ocht aye, now that is a big word for you, Doc!" Donald had recovered his composure.

"Get ti fuck yah wee…"

"Ocht well now here, what about you, Scully? Are you ever going to tie the knot with Angie, that's a wee while now?"

Before I could reply, Robbie interrupted. "Here does anyone else sense a touch of irony in the fact that one of the best mates of the worlds biggest Rolling Stones fan is shacked up with a girl called Angie?"

I swiftly changed my expression from open-mouthed to broad grin, and pointed cheerfully at Doc. "Aye Robbie first thing he asked me when I told him her name was 'Oh really Scullo... Now tell me do her kisses still taste sweet?" Doc shrugged to indicate that this was a perfectly reasonable question as I continued.

"Actually, you know the first time I met her as soon as I heard her name was Angela I just got this huge grin on my face, eh... cause of Doc here. So she's looking at me with a kinda what the fu... *has this guy been smoking* look about her. So, I had to explain how I would be able to remember her name nae bother. Then, I told her all about this!" I swept my arm in a languid arc to indicated the Bothy and surrounds. "She was really interested, so I said I'd show her some photos and well that's kinda how it all got started, now we're happily living together."

"Ocht now, you showed her photos of US... and that got you into her pants; I think we may be due a commission of some sort!"

"Aye," Doc taunted me gleefully.

"Well," I tried to look suitably aloof as I retorted, "for one thing she is slim, so not your type, Doughboy, and besides Doc, I'm pretty damn sure it wasnae any of the photos of *you* after three days without a wash that sealed the deal!"

"So, here at what point did you suggest, 'let's spend the night together,'" Robbie asked his question with a stifled chuckle.

"Aye there was nae rush, young Robbie, I just reminded myself that," as cheerfully I broke into song, "Ti..i..i...ime is on my side, yes it is..."

"Ocht fer," grumbled Donald, "Could we please stop with the strolling bones lyrics? Anyway, here I'm actually pleasantly surprised to hear that you finally settled down, Scully."

"Eh... how's that?" I frowned suspiciously.

"Well as a man who has followed his bell-end throughout his youth wherever and whatever that may lead him into."

"Oh hey c'mon, I wasnae nearly as bad as Banjo." I tried to inject a suitably indignant tone into my somewhat defensive retort.

"Ocht now Scully, I can easily list any number of scrapes you and your fondness for the fairer sex has gotten you *and* us into on many an occasion."

"Acht bollocks!"

"Eh... Flock of Seagulls?"

"Hey that wasnae just me!"

"Here what's that all about then?"

"Aye well see Robbie," Doc readily took up the tale, which elicited a glower from Donald, "One year we got the train up here the night before, plan was ti stop in Fort Bill and get the early southbound in the morning. We had a few cans on the train and when we got to Fort Bill headed out for a more. That's when Banjo and Scully managed to persuade two young ladies to accompany us back ti the youth hostel on the promise of more bevvy."

"I have to say they had a surprisingly weak constitution for Highland lassies."

"An' no' as woolly as your usual dates, Doughboy?"

"Feck off!"

"Aye, anyway, as Doughboy pointed out, weak constitution; now Scully here, having filled them with our good whisky, was engaged in some bedroom gymnastics wi' one lass when she took the urge ti vomit."

"Probably the sight of you naked, Scully."

"*Not* the usual reaction, I can assure you, young Robbie!"

Doc snorted, "aye right; anyway she launches it out the window on account of no' being able to make ti the bathroom!"

"Ocht aye, Scully here informed us the next day that he even tried to proceed after *that!*"

"Bent over, Robbie, naked butt winking at me and no need to smell her breath." I had held my arms open wide and tried to look angelic as I pled my case.

"Aye, but the worst of it was the following morning a gaggle of seagulls made one fuck of a racket fighting over the remains of her alcohol-soaked fish supper. This woke the caretaker, who upon investigation found out her mate having somehow resisted Banjo's charms had instead redecorated the bathroom. So he proceeded to boot us *all* out *way* too fuckin' early, told us never ti darken the door again."

"I still fail to see how it can be blamed on me!"

"Scully we ran out of whisky that year cause you and Banjo were plying it down the lassies' throats and then they threw it up."

"Acht your just jealous, Doughboy, cause her mate wasnae into yer Highland charms *or* your third eye."

"That has nothing to do with it!"

"What… wait a minute what's all this about a third eye?" Robbie was intrigued by my comment. Donald glowered furiously as Doc gleefully filled in the details.

"Doughboy here fell asleep during the party and Banjo drew a big eyeball on his forehead; we said nowt, and it was only when he got home that he noticed!'

"How did it take that long?"

"Ocht, it must have been the first time I'd taken off my hat near a mirror!"

"Well anyway that was then, me I'm happy enough these days; tell you what, we'll find a bar with sheep next time. Actually, hang on, did the Cyclops no' eat sheep?"

"Here now, there you go heh, changing the subject again; never mind me, what about that whisky?"

"Aye right enough, it was a waste of whisky Scully, just cause your claim is ti be a one women man these days doesnae absolve you!"

"'Absolve'? Fer fuck sake, Doc, who you been hanging' out with?"

"Aye, too much time listening ti you spouting yer ten bob words!"

"Oh, fuck aye Doc, whatever, ah need another cup of tea." It was clear the balance had shifted and they were both ganging up on me so I grabbed the kettle, but found it almost empty. "Hey we need water!"

"Ocht here I'll get it. I need a piss," Donald stood, stretched with a groan and reached for his boots. Suddenly the outside door slammed; it shook the Bothy walls as if an irate teenager had just ended an argument by storming out of the room. Doc was on his feet in an instant, knife in hand. A flurry of cups and cans clattered across the floor, as we scrambled to switch on head torches.

Breathing heavily, my heart pounding, I edged towards the door as Doc stood, arms out poised and ready. Slowly, I reached for the handle shifting my feet as I prepared to pull the door quickly open. Then, just as my hand gripped the cold metal doorknob a blast of icy air blew under the door, through the gaps around the ancient doorframe and the outside door slammed again.

Instantly, Doc relaxed; the tension fell off him. I pulled the door open and revealed a dusting of snow and sleet like someone had spilled a bag of sugar. It extended from the outside door into the corridor. The door creaked, swung gently on the wind and then slammed again.

"Who the fuck was the last one out?"

"Robbie!"

Doc grabbed the handle and pulled the outer door shut, then he twisted it several times. It emitted a shrill metallic squeak as the rusty mechanism slid into place. "Can you no' shut a door?"

"Acht... sorry lads!" Robbie exhaled a relieved sigh and returned to his seat, as Donald shook his head in reproach like a sorely disappointed parent.

"Here what were you going to do with that, Doc: Stab the ghost?" I pointed at the knife as Doc slid it back into its sheath.

"Fuck..." he laughed, "dunno!"

"Ocht well I *still* need a piss, but I will make sure the door is *shut* when I come back!"

6 THE JAKEY

A short time after Donald had returned the distinctive flash of a head torch was followed by the unmistakable jarring squeak of the outside door being opened.

.The wiry figure of our visitor stood at the doorway dripping, dressed head to toe in black Gore-Tex with a pair of army surplus leather boots. Switching off his head torch, he scanned the room breathing heavily, a rasping wheeze emanated from his throat.

"Alright Boyz?" the question rippled out in a nasal West Coast accent. His thin pointed face sported a large scar under the left eye and a good three days of stubble. The firelight unattractively enhanced the yellow hue of his crooked nicotine stained teeth.

"Aye no' bad, yourself?" I replied with a note of caution as I examined our visitor carefully.

"Fuckin' brand new now I found this place."

"Ocht now, here get yourself by the fire."

"Aye will do, ta," he nodded and scanned the room, "Four of yous... I'll drop my stuff in the wee room, grab a bunk, then come back and get warm."

He turned and pulled out a pack of cigarettes quickly lighting one as he headed out the door.

There was a short silence as we listened to his footsteps echoing down the hallway into the other room.

Using a slang term for natives of Glasgow I suggested, "Eh... a Weedgie perhaps?"

"Aye or even further West!"

"Seems alright?" Robbie glanced quickly at Doc for confirmation.

"Aye, looks like an extra fi 'Just a Boys Game' and nae mates an' all walking alone in the winter, choice or necessity?"

"Ocht now we shouldn't be so quick to..." Donald paused as footsteps grew louder and the door opened. The stranger had returned. He had swopped his jacket for a fleece and put on a woolen hat, both black. Donald shifted along the bench and made space.

The stranger placed four cans of Tennants Super Lager at his feet lit another cigarette and announced, "Jimmy," as he exhaled a cloud of smoke.

"Doc."

"Scully."

"Robbie."

"Donald."

"Fuck aye but we call him Doughboy."

"You want a Dram?" Robbie thrust out the whiskey and a plastic cup.

"Aye... don't mind if I do, eh... came o'er fi Culra!" Jimmy paused opened one of his beers, took a huge gulp and wiped his mouth with the back of his hand, "Pretty wild oot there the now; what about you boyz?"

"Eh... we came in from Rannoch this morning, this pair from Corrour."

"You fi Embra'," Jimmy narrowed his eyes and nodded curtly at me.

"Aye I am, him too," I flicked a thumb at Robbie.

"Aye the fuckin' posh voice gave it away, I'm fi Greenock," he offered, then nodded curtly at Doc.

"Scotstoun."

"Aye well, at least wan of yous is fi the West." Jimmy glowered at Donald out of the corner of his eye as he took several huge gulps from the can of beer, his scrawny throat pulsed in the firelight like a snake swallowing mice.

"Ocht me, I'm from the Black Isle originally, spent a few years in Edinburgh but I live on Arran these days."

"Ah a Teuchter, why'd yah move then, were the sheep starting to tell tales on yah?" Jimmy flashed his crooked yellow teeth in a grin, Donald just smiled weakly, clearly not amused.

"What's it you do then?" I decided to play nice even though Jimmy's abrasive manner was melting the relaxed atmosphere of the Bothy faster than snowflakes landing on the loch.

"Ticket inspector on the trains, fuckin' dawdle plenty time off, nea wan ever checks up on you."

"Aye?" Doc's voice sounded strangely neutral.

"Aye mainly Glasgae ti Embra' but I dinnae mind coming ti Embra' see me a've nae sense of smell." Jimmy's attempt at comedy was met with silence. "Whit about you?" he addressed Doc directly as if to indicate his intent to ignore the rest of us and only speak to those 'fi the West.'

"Mechanic," the one word response spoke volumes, he was going to have to work harder to get Doc to play nice.

"Aye, could you no have brought yer grease gun fur that fuckin front door?" Doc made no response so Jimmy attempted more humor, "So do you come here often, ladies?" again no response so he chuckled at his own joke and finished off his first can of beer. "Aye, actually prefer the wans further north; less likely ti bump inti English cunts."

"Aye like where?" I asked while I silently thought, 'and why the fuck did you no' go there then?'

"Sourlies or maybees Glenpean but I couldnae get the fuckin' time aff so I hit Culra, then headed o'er here."

"Anyone at Culra?"

"Naw was fuckin' empty, spent last night there on my own but see me I dinnae mind ma own company!"

Donald and I exchanged knowing glances at this information as Jimmy flicked his cigarette butt in the fire and fished around in his fleece for the packet. It occurred to me that Doc had not sworn for a least a minute, probably some sort of record, of course Jimmy was compensating adequately.

"Fuck getting warmer now," he announced pushing up his sleeves to reveal his sinewy tattooed arms. The crude tattoos were of the homemade variety achieved using a needle and ink. A badly drawn and indecipherable selection of daggers and skulls competed with a Greenock Morton Football Club crest. Under this was tattooed, 'The Pride of the Clyde' but the ink had merged, in the dim light the second word could easily have read 'Prick.'

"I'll head back ti Culra the morn, ah hid two more of these bad boys for the 'morrow night," he waved a can of super lager and added, "but I'll go round the fuckin' Ben, whit about yous?" again he pointedly addressed Doc.

"Up the Ben."

"Aye fuck been there done that," he sniffed and loudly cleared his throat spitting a huge gob of yellow phlegm at the fire, it missed and hit the guard then hung there and sizzled.

The full transformation was gradual, and probably took place around the sixth or seventh whisky Jimmy scrounged. Until then, he had been unpleasant, at least he started to engage all of us but mainly by expounding on any topic we discussed, offering his opinions. These ranged from 'aye that's fuckin' shite' to 'aye that's fuckin' pish' with particular vitriol reserved for members of the police, posh women, homosexuals and other ethnicities or in Jimmy's parlance the 'fuckin' filth, snobby cows, poofs, and the fuckin' English'. It soon became apparent that Jimmy hated and deeply mistrusted anyone who didn't live in or around Glasgow, drink like a fish, smoke like a chimney and shag any girl who would have him with the enthusiasm of a rabid dog. It was also clear that the solution to any impediment of Jimmy's lifelong pursuit of happiness was to either kick, slap or punch it into compliance.

Throughout the night Jimmy deftly managed to position himself directly in front of the fire, soaking up the available heat with his scrawny frame. He moved smartly enough when Doc returned to find him in his seat and growled 'would you steal ma fuckin' grave as quick?' But then as the whisky continued to flow and the Super Lager waned, he became downright obnoxious and our tolerance levels or more significantly Doc's patience rapidly diminished.

Jimmy offered his opinion yet again. "Fuckin' English poofs, just like yon cunts fi Embra'."

He reached out and grabbed a whisky bottle, poured himself a generous measure and quickly drank most of it chased down with a gulp of Super Lager. Robbie sighed and looked suitably aloof but Doc's eyes narrowed and his face darkened as he watched Jimmy helping himself, clearly, this act had finally crossed the line.

"Here, ah live in Edinburgh these days, I happen ti like it!"

"Acht well," Jimmy considered Doc carefully, "It no' so bad right enough, loads ah fuckin' money, eh? A while back I got a fuckin' braw new pack an' some gear fi a charity shop, tell you, Glasgae folk wouldnae chuck oot gear like that, quality!"

"Aye… which one?" Doc suddenly demanded, his face had darkened.

"Eh?"

"Which fuckin' charity shop?"

"Acht one in Gorgie cannae fuckin' mind which."

"When?"

"What's it fuckin' matter?"

"It fuckin' matters ti *me*." Doc replied softly and slowly his voice oozed with menace. His eyes flashed angrily and he casually moved so the knife handle on his belt became visible. Donald and Robbie sat up quickly, poised and ready, they'd heard the tone before, a storm was brewing. Suddenly with a sickening feeling in my stomach, I remembered the conversation at the lodge. Banjo's mum lived in Gorgie.

"Eh… well here, I've nae argument wi' you eh… big man!" Jimmy's eyes flickered rapidly between uncertainty and defiance as if he realized that he had overstepped some line in the sand, he just wasn't sure which.

"What gear was it?" Doc's teeth were gritted, the flickering light of the fire made it look like dark storm clouds were dancing across his brow.

"Hey Doc," we made eye contact for a moment and I shrugged my shoulders as if to say 'what you going to do, take it off him?' If Jimmy did have Banjo's stuff as Doc clearly suspected well he had come by it fair and square.

"Fuck eh… a pack, a jacket some boots thermals an' a nice wee stove."

Again the angry flash but then just as Doc opened his mouth as if to question further, Jimmy added, "Boots wur too big; same fur the jacket so I didnae take them."

"Aye," Doc relaxed visibly then added in a low growl, "Aye, they boots were too fuckin big for *you*, right enough!"

Jimmy now looked as confused as Donald and Robbie, to him the insult seemed unwarranted. "Ho, here steady now, we're all mates here right? Sorry if you Embra' cunts cannae take a joke."

"Oh, we can take a joke, you're just no' very fuckin' funny… pal," Doc pointedly missed out Jimmy's cup as he poured out more whisky.

Jimmy stared blearily into his cup sniffed, spat into the fire and huffily concluded, "ah well I guess that I'll do me for fuckin' East Coast hospitality then!" He finished his last beer and rose slowly to his feet.

Doc never took his eyes off Jimmy; he watched him like a hawk as he stomped nosily outside leaving behind a silent room filled only by the crackling noise from the fire.

"Fuck sake, *nine* percent ABV," Robbie shouted as he inspected one of Jimmy's discarded cans. "And he downed four of them, washing down his tramp juice with our good whisky!"

Doc exhaled; his shoulders sagged, but his eyes held fast on the door.

"Ocht he must have downed the best part of a bottle!"

"Fuck him, he'll no' be back," I nodded at the door, "He's no' that stupid, even a jakey bastard like that can count ti…" I stopped as the sound of doors being slammed shut announced that Jimmy had returned and gone into the other room.

"Better keep the ice axes handy, in case the wee bastard tries anything!"

"Ocht, well he'd have to climb over us to get to the whisky!"

"Right enough," I nodded at Doc, "Now that would be a suicide mission."

"Ocht here, what if he just slips in and slits our throats?" Donald made a comical face at Robbie his eyes wide.

"Tsk… aye, like all predators he'd go for the oldest and weakest in the herd first!"

"Aye or the slowest and fattest!"

"Ocht feck off you pair, now here Doc, I must say I can't see why you moved from Glasgow; such charming entertaining folks."

"Aye steady, Doughboy, Banjo's ma lives in Gorgie. Maggie said she took his gear ti a charity shop."

"WHAT, no feckin' WAY! You don't think…?" Donald looked shocked, "What are the chances?"

"Aye well, he's no' wearing his fuckin' boots at least!"

"Too big," Robbie nodded solemnly, suddenly Doc's odd comment had become clear.

"Acht fuck him! Anyway, here Doughboy there's plenty of radges fi Embra'."

"Ocht aye very true Doc and there's three of them sat right by this fire!"

"How the fuck's it three?"

Donald nodded at the plaque, "Ocht aye here, I was counting Banjo!"

7 TAKING UP GOLF

There were several minutes of noisy activity as the door crashed open and closed for a last piss of the night. We squeezed onto the platform, in order of arrival: Doc and myself at one end, Donald and the sleeping Robbie at the other.

"Hey stop shoving would you!" Robbie had been woken by Donald giving him a firm nudge.

"Stop taking up so much room then!"

"Its cause yer wearing wool Robbie yer getting him all excited."

"Ocht, feckin' comedians are we not, right zen," Donald slurred from his prone position "Band names with body parts, I'll start eh… Talking Heads!"

The contest was rapid fire at first, with names shouted out and rulings quickly made about the validity of each response.

"Heart!"

"Motorhead!"

"Stiff Little Fingers!"

"The Byrds!"

"Eh…?"

"Burdz have got body parts," I chuckled from deep in my sleeping bag.

"Fuck off; disallowed."

"Rolling Stones!"

"Totally predictable, Doc, but no slang terms." Donald admonished.

"The Faces, wi' out Rod."

"Captain Beef…heart!"

"Little Feat!"

"Buzz…cocks!"

"Waterboys,"

"No way, how's that?" demanded Doc.

"The body is eighty percent water, right Scully," he mumbled.

"Aye and about three percent whisky at the mo…" I slurred and quickly added, "Allowed."

"Radiohead!"

"Simple Minds!"

"The Tubes!"

"Flaming Lips!"

"Smash Mouth!"

"Butthole Surfers!"

"Slang." objected Robbie.

"Nine Inch Nails!"

"Aye, good one!"

"Tom Petty and the Heartbreakers!"

"Echobelly!"

"Golden Ear….ring!"

Gradually, the pauses became longer as we lay and racked our whisky-addled brains.

"Blackeyed Peas!"

"The Lemonheads!"

"The Shins!"

"Wishbone Ash!"

"Nickel…back!"

"Talking Heads!"

"We fuckin' had that at the start!"

"Aww…"

"Louis Arm-strong!"

"That's no' a band."

"Blood Sweat and Tears!"

Again silence, save for the crackling of the fire and the chilling sound of the wind as it howled past the door.

"Fuck, I need a piss!"

"Acht, could you no' have done that when everyone else did," I grumbled as Doc struggled out of his bag, pushed his feet into his boots, stomped across the floor and out the door. When he returned he dragged the Chesterfield over to block the door, kicked off his boots and climbed back into his sleeping bag.

"Acht we'll sleep better." he mumbled, "Anyway I can hear him snoring his head off; he's out for the count." His teeth chattered slightly as he added, "Fuck… but it's Baltic out there!"

Donald grunted something unintelligible and rolled over to find a more comfortable spot while Robbie now fast asleep, said nothing. Wide awake, Doc sat up, his sleeping bag around his waist, and watched the dwindling fire. Figuring sleep was not yet an option, I joined him as he lit a cigarette.

We sat in silence as the soft snores of Robbie competed with those of Donald. Doc turned to me and in a quiet voice asked, "So here, do you think you and Angie will ever tie the knot?"

"Eh… why, I mean why, what the, what do I need a piece of paper for Doc?" I was slightly taken aback, not like Doc to discuss such things, I concluded it must be the whisky then added with a chuckle. "Dinnae get me wrong though I'm really happy; she's eh... she's pretty special; kinda girl I can see myself putting together some playlists for!"

Doc's eyes narrowed thoughtfully at this information. In the silence of the Bothy, a candle flickered, its flame almost gone. The last few drops of wax had run down the wall over a slight protrusion and formed into an ornate stalactite.

"Did you get a chance to speak to Robbie?"

"Fuck nah, no' had a quiet moment, maybe tomorrow when we're on the hill; but besides, on the topic of fucked up relationships, I'm no' sure I'm the best one to be giving him any pointers. Things are still far fi' great at home for me. Ah mean its just gotten beyond eh... we've drifted, we were never the same anyway."

After this uncharacteristically heartfelt outburst, Doc fell silent and gazed morosely at the fire. "I dunno Scully, it just feels for a long time now, well the two total fuckin' strangers comment wasnae far off the mark. When we went back to the Glasgow for Crimbo I was all game on to see our old mates, have a pint and a laugh, all she wanted ti do was sit in front of the telly wi' a glass of bevvy n' my ma fur company."

I sighed and felt almost guilty, suddenly Doc seemed a little vulnerable not his usual pugilistic self, "Ah'm sorry to hear that, Doc, thought you might have turned it around that's a drag, man!"

"Aye, well, we all made our choices, nae second chances in this life right? Still I cannae help thinking sometimes when I look around that I might… *We* might have made a better choice," he sniffed loudly.

"Aye well, you've got to focus on the good times Doc!"

"There were *no* good times!"

"Must have been once, what about those wee bairns of yours? They're lovely!" I uttered the word lovely with genuine enthusiasm.

Doc shook his head, "aye probably the best thing ah' have ever done."

"Aye now see!"

"Acht… how do you do IT, Scully, eh…?"

"Do what?"

"Always have something positive ti say, see the bright side. I mean dinnae get me wrong. I'm no' complaining, ah just…" His voice trailed off and he looked at me questioningly.

"Aww I dunno, I've never really thought about it. Its just the way ah am. So... what are you going to do?"

"No sure, no' like I'm going ti find someone else," Doc rubbed his bald head ruefully, "Being young and good looking is no' wan of my problems!" He glowered sullenly into the firelight his shoulders slightly slumped.

"Oh fer fuck sake here, do you remember that afternoon at Hampden?"

"Fuck, which one?" he sighed.

Smiling, I began to describe a game at the National Football Stadium between Scotland and England. My voice developed a strange almost reverential tremor as if I was relaying some sort of mythical tale.

Stretching out an arm, I panned it slowly across the room, setting the scene. "It was a beautiful day, the air had that pollen-filled haze of summer, and the Hampden turf was an indescribable shade of green. The massed ranks of the Tartan Army had filled the stadium. It was just A SEA OF FLAGS; a solid blanket of Lion Rampants and Saltires. Their yellows and reds the blues and whites fluttered proudly over the heads of sixty thousand singing, chanting Scottish football fanatics."

My voice haltered, and with an exaggerated frown I whispered. "Then the English took the field and there in the center circle stood David Beckham, our own personal Bête Noire! Except of course, he was in white!"

My voice quivered slightly as I struggled to suppress laughter long enough to relay the story. Doc wore his best evil-looking broad grin as the memory came flooding back. He knew exactly what I was about to say; he had heard it before and would no doubt hear it a thousand times again and still laugh his arse off.

"*Then*, to a man the massed ranks started to sing, like the finest most perfectly harmonious Welsh Male Voice Choir, to the tune of that old Scottish spiritual!"

Doc snorted again as the tune in question was from an old British Airways advert called 'Fly the Flag'.

I began to softly sing the first line, "Ohh, Posh Spice takes it up the arse, Posh Spice takes it up the arse."

Doc joined in and as we sang together, our voices rose to a joyful crescendo.

"Ohhhhhh Posh Spice TAKES IT UH- UP THE ARSE!"

We repeated this joyful ditty three times, the crescendo rising higher with each rendition. As we finished, I had to wipe a tear of laughter from the corner of my eye, "Aye, fer sure it was one of the Tartan Army's finest ever aphorisms!"

"Eh... aye, whatever, Scully, you been chowing down on a dictionary again? Anyway here best part was all the police and security guys stood behind the goal in front of us were singing along an' all!"

I guffawed at this information, causing Donald to roll over and drowsily mumble, "Shut the feck up, you pair!"

We both sniggered, our heads together like a pair of wee boys, being scolded for talking in class. Then Doc's face became somber again, he exhaled a nasal sigh and growled. "Aye... but they still won!"

"Tsk... oh fer fuck sake, well, well what about King Kenny's goal against Spain then, eh...?"

"Which one?"

"The third one, I'll never forget that smile, pure one hundred percent proof undiluted joy!"

"Oh fuck aye, or when we trashed that shithole Wembley in 77!'"

"Aye well, before my time."

We sat and quietly reflected on these halcyon memories of Scottish football. Finally I broke the silence. "Aye, now see Doc its not that hard is it?" To me all life's problems seemed easily solved, simply by seeking out something to laugh about. The bar was never set that high, the prerequisite for continued good humor a mere mental Fosbury flop, using a simple recall of footballing pleasure.

"Aye, cheers for that Doctor Feelgood!"

"Nae bother my friend, take two a day and stay off the Leonard Cohen albums!"

"Oh fer fucksake! What the... why the Fu... am I listening to you anyway?"

"Eh... 'cause I know how to be cheerful yah grumpy wee shite," I laughed, "here tell me something Doc do you believe in reincarnation?"

"What?... Fuck, naw!"

"Aye well me I'm warming to the idea myself, I actually quite fancy coming back as a dolphin!" I announced this gleefully and looked triumphantly at Doc as if the concept of reincarnation was a fait accompli.

"Fer fuck sake Scully, have you been smoking that wacky baccy again!"

"Naw Doc fer fuck, eh... Dolphins are beautiful, sleek, graceful *and* decidedly intelligent mammals!"

"Aye wi a fuckin bottle fur a nose." Doc chortled happily at his own joke.

"Acht ti fuc'..." This time I sighed.

"Fer fuck sake Scully..." Doc growled, "I must seriously be off ma head. Aye, yah feckless nomad, dodging commitments, nae kids, nae plans ti get married! I'm looking ti you for advice!"

He had a point I had to chuckle at that, "Well you should ask Donald his advice then if you want a sensible answer. He seems to have cracked it, marriage that is."

Waving a hand, Doc growled, "Aye, right, here do you think you'd loose all that if you settled down?"

"All what?"

"Yer endlessly sunny attitude!"

"Ah well ah dunno, maybe, no do-overs though as they say in the States. We've all made our choices, anyway, I *do* know about commitment, I bought a Hearts season ticket, twice!"

"Oh fer fuck sake Scully well let's just say some of us are a wee bit more committed!" Doc shook his head ruefully

"Well maybe you should have thought about that before you sent out the swimmers," I laughed at the analogy before I added with my usual unbridled enthusiasm. "Bonnie wee bairns they turned out though, take after their Ma!"

"Aye *true*, but as I think I mentioned only when they're being nice and as I vaguely recall, my future life and long term happiness was actually the furthest thing fi my mind!"

"Aye well, see your minds no in the program at that time! Its been hijacked by the autonomic nervous system intent on reproduction. You were merely a pawn in its game. Putty in its hands, eh… actually," I held up a finger, "That, may no' be the very best of analogies."

"You dinnae half talk a load of total pish, Scully," Doc cut me off shaking his head wryly at my academic monologue.

"Aye, so what *are* you going to do?"

"Ah havnie got a Scooby Doo, cannae unscramble an omelette! It's a mess, *my fuckin' mess!*"

"You could take up golf, like other blokes our age! Spend your Sunday in the nineteenth hole getting pissed up and reliving past glories, famous putts I did or didnae hole!"

"As opposed to dragging our weary carcasses into Ben A and sharing our problems?" Doc twisted his face into a scowl at this statement.

"Well, if I had to choose between the two…." My face suddenly became serious, "aye fair point, next year I'll bring over my clubs!"

"Actually … an annual golf outing would be a doddle compared wi' getting a group of us here. Then there's the added achievement of doing this relatively peacefully even wi' all that whisky! Aye an that's wi' the best intentions of you and Doughboy trying ti wind each other up and start a wee rammy."

"Eh… wait a minute*,*" I was indignant, *"me;* he seems to have been getting your back up as per usual!"

"Aye well ah can always tell wi you Scully you *start* calling him Doughboy!"

"Acht well cannae help that! That's like a great big button on his forehead that says 'push here'!" I jabbed my finger at an imaginary button to emphasize the point.

"Fuck aye, well we all have one, its just more visible ti some than ti others." Doc's tone suddenly became serious. "Here, you know what… you're really lucky, you know that, Scully?"

"Aye how's that?"

"Acht… fuck," he sighed and shook his head.

I knew what he meant, I scanned the Bothy, the prone figures of Robbie and Donald, the dying fire, all while listening to a wind that howled and rattled the door, finally I responded. "Aye, I suppose you're no' wrong my old friend, I mean we could be stuck on the back nine someplace with the wrong clubs!"

With a loud snort, Doc slid down into his sleeping bag and shook his head gently. A soft crackle filled the silence; the dying fire pulsed in an orange glow filling the darkened room like the light from a jack-o-lantern. The last candle flickered and a brief glint of light served as a reminder of the brass plaque on the mantle.

"I really miss Banjo, you know," I followed the statement with a heavy sigh. "I never thought we'd do this again."

"Aye… well were no' getting any younger, I wonder how many years he would have managed ti motivate us for?"

"He never would have stopped in a way," I nodded at Robbie's prone figure, "would've just passed the torch."

"Aye fer fuck, he saw a different side of Banjo did he no'?"

"Acht I dunno Doc, think he was just getting mellow, maybe less to prove to Robbie."

I plumped up the bivvy sack pillow filled with spare clothes, snuggled down, pulled on my hat and tightened the drawstring to keep out cold drafts. Doc closed his eyes as he waited for sleep to come get him. I stared silently as shadows danced across the ceiling and reflected on the day. Just then, Doc's head lolled gently, his mouth inches from my ear.

He began to snore.

Outside in the night, the wind reined in its fury and gradually dropped to a gentle breeze like a soft cool whisper. As the door stopped rattling I drifted off to sleep, carried on waves of guttural snores. Amidst the crackle and throbbing pulse of dying embers the stove clanged lightly as it slowly cooled. The wind breathed a final sigh. The last few clouds dissipated and the relatively warmer air began to rise from the ground into a cold clear sky. For a short time, a waxing crescent moon and an infinitesimal number of stars illuminated the icy coating of the crooked slate roof.

Then a mist began to form.

As it crept down then glen it seemed to probe and feel its way. It coated the land, wrapped gently around the Bothy covering everything in a silent fluffy white shroud.

8 BRASS PLAQUE

I woke first, fumbled in the semi-dark for my head torch, shrugged on warm clothes, pushed my feet into my boots and hobbled stiffly to the door. Dragging the Chesterfield to one side I stepped into the hallway, the noticeable drop in temperature enveloping me, stripping away the relative warmth and humidity of the room. A hard tug on the outer doors released them from their frame; they twisted and resonated for several seconds like weird primitive musical instruments. I left them hanging in the cold air, as they called out their mournful dawn reverberations.

The cold grey light of a Highland dawn greeted me. The wind that had howled the previous night had dropped to nothing leaving the loch surface dark, still and silent. The snow-capped ridge of Sgor Gaibhre and the western flank of Ben Alder had gone, cloaked by a low white blanket of clouds. There was almost complete and utter silence, nothing, not a whisper. Soon the loudest noise by far was from a steady stream of urine hitting the icy ground. Shifting my balance slightly, I leant on one leg, let out a long slow fart, and eased my stance with a satisfied sigh.

"Fer fuck sakes, Scully, you're like a toxic cloud!" Doc's voice hoarse from whisky and cigarettes croaked through the silence and echoed across the loch.

"Alright Doc, didnae hear you come out; how you doing?"

"Am no' surprised wi' that racket," he nodded curtly, "aye, fine!"

I had a silent laugh at that, 'aye fine' as in we shall not speak of last night and any whisky-induced signs of emotional weakness.

I stepped back and scanned the low cloud. My leggings had no pockets so I casually thrust my hands down the front and stood, cradling my balls, feeling their warmth. "Fuck all view from the top of the Ben today!"

"Aye fuck it, kettle's on!"

"You'll have your usual triple mocha with soymilk and a dash of Belgian chocolate?" I made the suggestion knowing full well what the response would be, then stomped off in a slightly bow-legged manner back to the Bothy.

"Aye fer fuck," Doc paused and farted before adding, "as long as it's a grande!"

❖

The sound of the kettle boiling had roused the others and they soon filled the Bothy with a dawn chorus of farts and groans.

"Ocht fer feck, that *is* rotten; something has crawled up your arse and died," Donald glowered accusingly at Robbie as a pungent aroma hit his nostrils.

"I'm just getting my revenge on whoever took a shit in my mouth during the night," Robbie grimaced as he ran his tongue round his teeth.

"Aye that was me," the response came quickly and in perfect unison from three other voices.

"Oh…ho there goes our pal Jimmy!" I watched him as he walked past the window, shovel in hand.

"Wanker," grumbled Robbie taking a tentative sip out of a steaming cup of tea, his face abruptly contorted as he grimaced in disgust. "Fer fuck sake, did you wash that cup out?"

"What, wash cups? Now, you shouldn't have left whisky in it, should you, you soft Southern lightweight! Besides that will put hair on your chest!"

The first word of the standard response couplet had formed on Robbie's lips when the door crashed open. Doc burst in his face red with rage waving a bottle of whisky. "Fuckin' wee jakey!"

"*Where* did that come from?"

"Next door, wee jakey bastard was holding out on us drinking all our whisky; I went ti check, I'm pretty sure *it is* Banjo's pack. Then I looked inside for a name tag and saw *this,* what a total fucker,"

Doc stared darkly at the whisky bottle, which I fleetingly reflected, was not the usual manner he gazed upon such receptacles. Then his face abruptly changed, he had clearly had a moment of revelation. "Here, Robbie, quick get the pouch o' that piss-awful whisky," He barked the instruction as he snatched an empty plastic bottle from the shelf and swiftly emptied the contents of Jimmy's bottle into it. "Doughboy go keep an eye out, he's gone for a dump, tap on the window if you see him coming back!"

"Ocht aye, no bother!" Donald darted out.

"Hang on, gi'es that," Robbie pulled down the front of his leggings and started to piss into the whisky bottle, "Nae sense of smell eh… well here's some added warm Embra' hos-piss-tality!"

"Dinnae overdo it!"

"That ought to be enough," Robbie held the bottle firmly on the shelf as Doc topped it off with the contents of the pouch and replaced the cap.

"Oh what a lovely colour," he enthused as he held it up to the light, tapped on the window, gave Donald the thumbs up and darted through to replace the bottle.

A frying pan had replaced the kettle above the roar of flickering butane by the time Jimmy returned. He pointedly ignored us staying in the other room as he enjoyed a hearty breakfast of a cup of tea and a cigarette, the latter hung out the corner of his mouth while he packed his gear. He slammed the door as he left and coughed loudly to half mask a shout of 'wankers' as he past the window. There was no vocal response, we just stood and grinned then wandered outside and watched with mixed emotions as Jimmy's scrawny figure bearing Banjo's old pack dwindled into the distance.

"He is going to be *very* unhappy when he cracks that open," Robbie chuckled.

"Acht he's a *jakey* he'll no' even notice!"

"Ocht I'm not sure, that stuff was nasty!"

"Aye, well Robbie here even put a wee but extra gold in it, Donald, it's a new drink we're calling it Pissky."

"Aye, marching up the glen with a bottle of piss n' whisky."

"Now you know what boys? That could only improve it!"

"Told you it would come in useful for an emergency! Robbie was grinning broadly clearly feeling exonerated. "Here, do you think he'll come back when he finds out?"

"Aye maybe, long way ti walk for a punch in the mouth and a kick in the baws though!" Doc cleared his throat loudly, spat in the direction of the departing Jimmy and headed back into the Bothy.

The thick slices of black pudding sizzled noisily as Doc threw in some back bacon and opened up a pink plastic lunch box that sported a 'Dora The Explorer' logo.

"What ya' got in there then, Doc?" Robbie grinned gleefully at the box.

"Unicorn shit!" growled Doc as he cracked two eggs on top of the concoction. He pierced the yolks and watched as the liquid flowed into the gaps, spitting, bubbling, solidifying, as it turned yellowy-white.

I stood poised holding open a pitta bread, watching proceedings closely with a concerned look on my face. There was no chance any of us would eat anything if it fell on this floor: we had our standards. We needn't have worried; deftly splitting the contents of the frying pan into four roughly equal portions, Doc shoveled a portion of the greasy concoction into the waiting mouth of the open pitta bread. It slithered in like a snake without a morsel being spilt. I handed it swiftly to Donald and opened another.

"Why thank you, sir," adding Tabasco and pepper, he took a huge bite out of the steaming masterpiece, the grease oozing out and running between his fingers. "Ocht aye... just the job," he enthused, "here, now anyone feeling a little hungover?"

"Aye, but no' so bad, Donald, no' so bad! Here, at least I'm no' seeing any large chickens!" We chuckled as we enjoyed our shared joke.

"What the fu...."

"Ocht here, aye! Banjo was in *some* state that day. As I recall, he came straight from a party, so he must have been up all night smoking, bevvying and flirting with the ladies! Straight to the bar and cracked back onto the booze, he could hardly stand by the time we got to the game."

"Aye, well, that seems to have been standard Banjo form, but here, what's all this about a chicken, then?" Robbie had grasped the latest artery-hardening offering thrust towards him.

"Aye, well see, this was a New Year's Day game between Hibs and Hearts. First half was a total bore, though Hearts were of course the better team," I added the provocative taunt to irritate Robbie.

"Indubitably," quipped Donald.

"Total pish," was Robbie's curt, knee-jerk retort mumbled through a mouthful of bacon and egg.

"Now see, this was back in the days of terracing, so there's about twenty -five thousand hungover, eh... actually still drunk supporters, chanting the usual obscenities. Now presumably to keep us from hurling rocks, coins and beer cans filled with piss at each other, the authorities decided to supply us with some half-time entertainment."

"Oh aye, very good like yon Superbowl then, Scullo, the Stones maybe?"

"Eh... almost but not quite spot on, Doc! No, in their infinite wisdom, the Powers That Be decided that only *one* thing would keep the drunken and hungover hordes distracted from thoughts of violence and mayhem. That being the awe-inspiring spectacle of some complete arse, dressed as an eight foot high chicken taking penalty kicks against a schoolboy goalkeeper!"

"Ahhh... fuck, quality entertainment, for sure! Now tell me, did that work?"

"Acht... I've paid more attention to a Tory politician making a conference speech. In fact, we were all paying absolutely *no* attention whatsoever, which is kind of the gist so to speak of the tale. We just continued chanting about how much we all hated each other; they sang their songs, we sang ours." I juggled two pittas, one with a crescent-shaped bite, waiting as Doc switched off the stove. "Aye, but then suddenly Banjo, who was stood just behind us, weaving unsteadily, becomes mightily concerned. See, he decided that what he was seeing on the pitch was actually a manifestation conjured up by the old 'delirium tremens'. So he blurts out in a shaky terrified voice, "Here… lads, can anyone else see a big fuckin' chicken taking penalties?" Of course, we all kept quiet and tried to look nonchalant and pretend we could see nothing."

"Ocht aye, he was shitting his pants!" Donald added as he meticulously licked the grease from his stubby fingers.

"Then," my voice quivered slightly I was having difficulty suppressing my laughter, "All of a sudden this half-eaten pie comes arcing out of the crowd!" I gesticulated wildly making an exaggerated arc with my right arm, "and BOOM it makes a direct hit; it just explodes on the side of the chicken's head! Of course, we all burst out laughing because the chicken, it goes down as if it's been taken out by sniper fire. Then this huge cheer goes up as the ambulance boys advance with the stretcher, but the chicken just rips his own head off and storms angrily from the field."

"A headless chicken!"

"Indeed, but of course by then, the ruse was up as Banjo swiftly realized the whole debacle was actually not a figment of his alcohol addled imagination. He had a mighty relieved look on his face like a man who had just been told by his doctor that actually, it was okay to drink again!"

"Ocht aye, totally unbelievable!"

"Unbelievable, I thought you said you where there!"

"Aye I was, I just could not believe anyone would throw away a perfectly good pie!"

Robbie shook his head ruefully, sipped from his tea and stooped to look out the window. "Brightening up, yup looking good, nae rain that's all I care about. Right then, enough trips down the memory lane that is Scottish football, when we going up Ben Alder?" He slammed down his tea emphatically, stretched and easily touched his toes. Suddenly, he realized his vulnerability and turned sharply to find Doc behind him, with a big grin on his face.

"Fuck, I was about ti kick you right up the arse, you rubbery bastard!"

"It's called being fit, you old fart, just 'cause all your temple of a body is used for these days is turning bevvy into piss and curry into shite."

"Old fart, is it? Cheeky wee fuck! Hey, you two, hold him down while I get the poker," Doc advanced menacingly towards Robbie.

"Ho, children, children," Donald laughed, "Here, cut it out, kettles boiled anyone for more tea? Where's your mugs?"

At this invitation, Robbie sat on the bench and grinned as he took one of the mugs. A flurry of activity followed as clothes, food, and beverages were prepared for the day's hike. Then as he wandered casually past, Doc satisfied his need for retribution by farting right in Robbie's face.

"Away to fuck, yah dirty…" Robbie howled at the departing Doc, who, laughed manically as he headed outside, shovel clutched in one hand.

When Doc returned he held a small flat rock he had selected from the stream. He grabbed the plastic bag from the mantelpiece and growled. "Right ti fuck, let's do this job first before we head up the Ben for the *main* event, it'll no' take long!"

Donning our jackets and hats we shuffled outside and began inspecting the porch for a suitable spot.

"How about here?" Donald pointed to an area to the right of the door, sheltered from the wind and rain.

"Aye," I pointed to the spot where we had sat and enjoyed our tea the previous night, "The evening sun hits about here."

"Aye well that'll do then," there was a general murmur of consent as we each inspected the spot. Doc held the plaque against the wall, "Here or higher?"

"Naw there, that's perfect!"

"Maybe eye level."

"Your eyes or mine?"

"Ocht lanky big bastard!"

"Fuck's sake, its going *here*!" He carefully hammered in the first couple of nails, stepped back and checked the edge was straight. Satisfied, he hammered in the remaining nails, tapping them deep into the wood.

Now secured firmly to the wall, the simple brass plaque read.

IN MEMORY OF JOHN 'BANJO' BROWN
A FINE FRIEND ON THE HILLS AND BESIDE A BOTHY FIRE
HE LOVED THIS PLACE!

"Aye great job Doc," I said enthusiastically, "really nice, very fitting!"

"That looks great," Robbie was fiddling with his camera.

"Aye I wanted ti put 'he fuckin' loved this place' but ah was overruled!"

"Ocht it reads just fine as is!"

"Aye he'd have approved I suppose, job one done," Doc tapped a nail head one last time and gently wiped the brass surface as we headed back into the Bothy to prepare for the climb, up Ben Alder.

9 EAGLES AND HARRIERS

As he strode quickly ahead of us, Robbie seemed to climb the steep path effortlessly. Strung out in a silent line, we followed, heads bowed, breathing deeply, ascending into the mist.

The silence of the hills soon became absolute, broken only by the occasional guttural cry from a startled grouse or the sharp haunting call of a raven. I counted softly, in time with the rhythmic crunch of my footsteps, then stopped when I reached a hundred to catch my breath. Bent over, hands on my knees taking deep breaths, I could feel the slow steady throb of my pulse as the previous night's toxins distilled on my forehead in glistening beads of sweat.

We paused after maybe an hour, the Bothy and its backdrop, the loch and the tongue of land sparsely covered with trees where we had collected wood still visible through the low cloud. Robbie set up his camera, balanced precariously on a rock. As a red light flashed, he took a few leaping strides down the hill to join us and shouted. "Quick, say cheese!"

Donald and I turned to look with frozen awkward half-smiles while Doc kept his back to the camera as a loud click announced the moment had been recorded.

"Ho… check it out!" Doc pointed, a golden eagle soaring past us less than fifty feet away, its talons tucked out of view, its menacing-looking beady black eyes watching us closely.

"Death on the wing," I watched and tracked the eagle's flight. It screamed, offended by our intrusion, a strange haunting sound that echoed and reverberated like an ancient battle cry, sending a shiver down my spine.

"Aye for fuc…" Robbie scrambled back and furiously fiddled with the camera, "Aww shite," he wailed as the raptor soared gracefully into the mist.

"Ho say fuckin' cheese… eagle!" Doc laughed mockingly.

As we passed the bealach and climbed on up the steep flank of Ben Alder, the snow developed a hard icy crust. As Robbie led, he kicked in his toes making small steps. I followed, kicking at the same spots or hacking with my ice axe to increase the indent. It was exhausting work, and after a couple of hundred steps, we moved aside to let Donald and Doc take over.

The relay process carried on for almost an hour until a large rock face loomed out of the mist. Robbie propelled himself up a steep snow-filled gully, hacking with his axe, sending showers of ice cascading down the gully that tinkled like broken glass. I caught me breath and watched Donald and Doc's slow progress below as Robbie eased himself further up through the narrowing gap.

Suddenly out of the mist Robbie's voice cried out shrilly. "*Fuck me!* Get up here now, boys, you *are not* going to believe this!"

His voice seemed to echo through the silence of the gully. We exchanged quizzical glances then kicked furiously into the steps above us and moved upwards rapidly. Moments later, we stood next to Robbie, foreheads glistened with sweat, as we dug out sunglasses and joined in with his joyful expletives.

We had emerged onto a rocky outcrop at the top of the gully and climbed through and above the misty clouds. Now we stood above a gently undulating blanket of fluffy white that seemed to cover all of Scotland. The swearing stopped and we just stared in awed silence. The sky above us was an impossible shade of cobalt blue and the noonday sun glinted and sparkled off the ice crystals in the snow beneath our feet. The pristine white sea of clouds was breached far to the south by the distinctive cone-shaped summit of Schiehallion. It poked through like the tip of a wizard's hat,; to its right sat the squat summit of Garbh Mheall, puffy and white like an overgrown marshmallow. Instead of huge mountains, both peaks now seemed like distant islands on a white sea in some magical fairytale kingdom. To the northwest, a hundred or so feet above us stood the southern peak of Ben Alder: stark, unspoiled, and gleaming white; without sunglasses the glare from the crystal-flecked snow would have been blinding.

I grabbed my video camera and tried to capture the panorama as Robbie resumed climbing to the southern summit, kicking up showers of ice, which cascaded and formed fleeting rainbows. He turned, pulled out his camera and quickly snapped a few shots, freezing our euphoric grins for perpetuity. Then, still elated, he crunched on upwards, reverently soaking up the view as he crossed the icy ground to the top of the snow-capped peak.

Here the route dropped, and traversed a small saddle leading to the main summit. On our right, a large cornice of snow and ice formed a treacherous overhang above an eight-hundred-foot drop. The clouds seemed to break on this like waves on a snow-covered beach. However, the snow also covered almost all trace of rocks, which might demark the edge where the flimsy cornice became unable to support our weight.

"Eh..." Donald was about to urge caution but stopped as I pushed to the front and took a very conservative loop, well away from the danger of the cornice.

As we approached the main summit, we could see the peaks of Aonach Beag and Geal Cairn separated from us by a short channel in the sea of churning clouds. Far to the northwest, the distinctive summit of Ben Nevis danced in the sunlight shimmering and white it towered over its companion peaks from the nearby Ring of Steall.

We strode eagerly on and reached Ben Alder's broad flat summit just after midday. The large cairn of stones that surrounded the plinth was coated in ice that had been whipped and sculpted by the constant winter wind into a frozen horizontal waterfall.

Robbie rummaged through his pack for his lunch hesitating briefly as he felt a familiar shape. Frowning he pulled out a can of McEwans Export. "How the *fuck* did you do that? I thought I'd checked my pack!"

"Ocht now... there should be two!"

We sat on our packs in the brilliant sunshine and munched on tuna sandwiches. We argued about the names of the distant floating peaks, each debate resolved quickly and categorically with map and compass.

"Now this," I declared slowly, "Is worth the price of that ticket!"

"Aye this will keep me coming back for more," Robbie agreed enthusiastically.

"Oh fuck, aye!" Doc nodded happily.

"Amazing," Donald sounded breathless, "I've seen a few temperature inversions in my time but never one this total! Absolutely stunning!"

"Magical, totally! Hey, if we had a cloud boat we could sail from here over to Annoch Beag."

"What in fuck a *cloud* boat?"

"You know, I was thinking of something like a Viking longship with us at the helm floating majestically across, maybe a bunch of Amazonian babes at the oars." Robbie rubbed his hands and grinned enthusiastically.

"*Aye?* Here, Robbie is it fuckin' lonely on yer planet?"

"Away to fuck with you Doc, you you've nae imagination."

"He used to have, back in his magic mushroom days,"

Robbie clearly wasn't going to let Doc's cynicism spoil his enjoyment, ""Aye, well, anyway, that was some photo of you boys earlier, like a bunch of wee boys in a sweetie shop, so you were! Now then, time for another Kodak moment, I reckon!"

We shuffled to our feet happily enough, willing to try and capture the moment for posterity. Robbie looked through the viewfinder and motioned as he tried to get us lined up. "Doc, could you go a wee bit further to yer left so I can see the top of Ben Nevis past your fat bald head."

"Acht, fuck off," he responded without the slightest trace of animosity.

Behind us, the undulating blanket of white cloud was interspersed with almost pure white peaks with just a hint of darker patches here and there, rocky outcrops onto which even the snow could not cling. I looked around at the contented smiles. Doc was grinning, not his mean smile at some poor sod's misfortune or even a gleeful gloat; no. it was a happy grin: ecstatic, carefree, maybe even youthful. We did not have a care in the world.

Setting the timer, Robbie declared. "Say chee eh… temperature inversion!"

We held our grins easily as the loud click declared the recording of the moment no doubt to be reproduced one day perhaps on film or digitally. Dusted off, pulled from an album, or shown on a phone screen. Perhaps it would be presented and patiently explained to a child or an elderly relative, a trophy that recalled our fleeting presence in one of the high, wild places of the world, yet inadequate and incapable of conveying the feeling of the moment. No, this would be a shared memory, one that was cherished like a peaty dram of finest malt, savoured time and again in company of similar minds, huddled around a warm and smokey Bothy fire.

"Right then," Doc reached for his pack, "One more job ti do, time ti send Banjo on his way, *fuck it* but he would have loved this day! Eh… here, Maggie asked if we could get some pictures, Robbie?"

"Aye nae bother, let's see now if you all stand there, I'll get the sun behind me, eh… where will we scatter him?

"Near the summit I suppose; that's what he asked for," Doc began ripping off duct tape from a plastic bag to reveal another can of McEwans Export. A modified can, the top carefully cut off and re-attached, with a line of epoxy resin.

"No fuckin' way, is he in *there*?" Robbie pointed at the can, mouth wide in shocked disbelief.

"It seemed appropriate!"

"Totally, considering the amount of cans he'd had in him over the years!" I was trying hard not to laugh at Robbie's horrified expression.

"Ocht here you didn't show that to Maggie, did you?"

"Naw she gave me the urn; it was a big heavy thing I wasnae carting that in so I eh… repotted him, managed no' ti get him all over my workbench."

"Robbie I really don't think he would have been offended in the least, after all it was his favorite beer!"

The shocked look was frozen on Robbie's face but I was damn sure Banjo would actually have totally approved.

"Well fuck it, there wasnae anything else in my house!"

"Plus you got to drink the beer and check for gold teeth!"

"Ho… steady Scully this is a somber occasion."

"Eh… it might be said that you're kind of ruining the gravitas." I nodded at the offending can.

"Well I dunno Doc," Robbie pouted and looked unhappy.

"Ah ti' fuck c'mon its only ashes after all!"

"Aye well, I suppose," Robbie shrugged and fiddled with his camera.

"Ocht here Robbie get the angle right, so Maggie just sees the ashes and not the can?"

"Aye, okay."

"Here, there's hardly a breath of wind; we'll scatter him over this way."

"Maybe down a bit slightly off the summit, we can come back in the summer and see if the grass is a bit greener."

"Tsk… always the fuckin' scientist." Doc growled as he twisted the can sharply, the top came off easily. "You ready then, Miss Leibovitz?"

"Aye!"

"Anyone want ti say something before aye, ah?"

"Eh… aye," Robbie coughed and cleared his throat. "You'll no get any older pal, unlike us lot. No more getting knackered just easy sailing. Now when ever we have a wee nip or our morning cup of tea, well we'll think of you Banjo!"

"Ocht here very nice, Robbie, now where did that come from?"

"Eh… it's an adaption."

"Aye well, very touching, you could bring a tear ti a glass eye, so you could. Now, you ready?"

Robbie nodded and readied the camera as Doc carefully tipped the can spilling the grey white ash into the brilliant sunshine. A cloud of lighter ash floated, swirling on an imperceptible breeze as the heavier particles quickly coated the snow and exposed rock. There was total silence save for the sound of Robbie's camera as it clicked furiously. Shaking the last of the ash out of the can as Robbie took more shots and we stood silently watching the dusty cloud float gently down.

"Should we eh… cover him up with snow?"

"Ocht no, let him enjoy the view, Robbie!" Donald pulled out a hip flask and poured a circle of golden liquid into the middle of the ashes, his voice cracked slightly as he softly mumbled, "Slainte Banjo, Slainte!"

"Aye, what a beautiful day, it's perfect, we couldnae have asked for better!"

"Aye well photo's look good… oh, better delete that, got the can in it!"

"Just as well I dinnae fancy trying ti pick him up and do it again! Anyway ti fuck, c'mon I'm getting cold, standing around here."

"Here it looks, eh… he looks, like a map of Scotland," I pointed at the ashes, they had formed into an almost perfect shape.

"So it does, look that rock even looks like the Grampians; how did you do that Doc?"

"Eh… I'm no' seeing that; what the fuck have you boys been smoking?" Doc tilted his head one way then the other, "Now c'mon, cloud boats and maps o' Scotland, what a bunch. Now, which way shall we head down?"

A short debate began as to the best route to take. One choice would be to drop down into the glen between us and Gael Cairn. That route would pick up the very path that Donald and Robbie had joined the day before, rising up from Loch Ossian. It was a longer choice, as the path curved slowly down the glen, but we would make good time. An alternative shorter route would retrace our steps and descend much more precipitously, but that way was icy, and could be tricky underfoot.

"We'll no' get a better day then this out on the hills, the more time we have the better!" Doc emphatically resolved the short discussion.

Suddenly, Robbie pointed to the northwest: The lower flanks of Gael Cairn had started to appear. "Shite, it's breaking up!"

I looked around and noted sadly that the world was once more encroaching on our floating cloud top sanctuary. The temperature had risen sufficiently and as a light wind moved the clouds, the lower regions of other peaks began to appear. "Great while it lasted and perfect for sending Banjo on his way!"

"Ocht aye, you're not wrong there!"

"Here, we should write this up in the Bothy book, let all those who follow and get caught in a whiteout with zero visibility know what weather *we* had!" Robbie chuckled.

We packed up quickly and Donald graciously offered to carry the now-empty cans of beer. Robbie nodded at the ashes as he slung on his pack, "Feels strange to be leaving him here."

"Aye well we'll be joining him if we hang about any longer in this cold, now c'mon," Doc growled, and with that parting comment off we trudged safe from the danger of the cornice, across the broad sloping back of Ben Alder towards Gael Cairn.

For once Robbie did not take the lead, but instead hung back, seemingly sorting out his gear. I turned and noted with a disappointed shake of my head that he was surreptitiously checking his phone. As he waited for it to spring into life, he stared across the gradually dissipating sea of cloud at the towering massive of Anoch Beag, where I had once had a signal. Clearly, the top corner of Robbie's screen was giving a different story, reluctantly he replaced his phone and strode rapidly to join the group.

"Ho check it out!" Doc shouted pointing down the side of the steep ridge, "It's a Brocken Spectre!"

We moved quickly to the spot where Doc stood, the angle of the sun was perfect as it shone from directly behind us and cast his shadow on the clouds. The projected shadow looked enormous and it was surrounded by a circular rainbow like a halo as light refracted in the water droplets. There was an almost perfect angle and if we stood close together, we could form a double shadow with a single rainbow. Taking turns we danced around waved our arms and laughed in delight at the distortive effect we had on the huge colorful optical illusion.

Although fascinating we soon tired of this game and moved on, the low winter sun might have given light at a perfect angle, but it gave little heat.

Robbie had lagged behind, "Whoa," he shout brought us to an abrupt halt.

"What the... what's up?"

"That was weird."

"What was?"

"It was like there was an extra one," He looked sharply to his right as if he expected to see one of us.

"Acht, there cannae be *two* Robbie, the angle has to be perfect the sun directly behind you playing onto the cloud; someone has to stand right next to you!"

Robbie moved back up the slope his gaze fixed on the cloud borne illusion, it had faded as the sun moved away from its perfect angle. He shook his head, "That was weird; I swear for a fleeting moment I saw two rainbows!"

"Acht c'mon ti fuck," shouted Doc as he headed purposefully down the hill.

An hour or so more of walking and the broad back of the Ben turned into its steep flank as the ground dropped sharply. We took huge strides down the sloping, north east-facing flank of the mountain, at times hitting regions of almost waist-deep sugary snow.

"Here, which genius had this idea then?" Donald shouted breathlessly as he extricated himself from a waist-deep patch and moved arms outstretched, ready for the next precipitous drop.

"Ah stop yer moaning, old man," Robbie swiftly paid for the comment when a good-sized snowball hit the back of his head. "Oi, fuck off you old bastards," he countered, unsure of which one of us had thrown the snowball.

It was then that he realised his disadvantage. For once, his fitness was a detriment; as usual, he had moved faster and was now twenty or thirty feet below on an extremely steep slope in deep snow. His valiant attempts to fling snowballs upwards were unproductive. He laughed and swore in equal measure as he desperately tried to avoid the icy missiles, which exploded on or all around him. The successful hits and there were many, were met by roars and cheers from the pursuing band of assailants. Fortunately for Robbie, we soon tired of this sport, but not until one last looping throw from Doc resulted in a snowball that burst with an invigorating chill down the back of Robbie's neck. His anguished howl of pain only succeeded in generating a loud and derisory cheer of joy from the 'old bastards.'

By the time we reached the path, the undulating blanket of clouds had been reduced to a few snake-like tendrils. These extended in wisp-like vapour trails as if from a jet engine and hung motionless in the middle of the glen. We caught up with Robbie and nodded in acknowledgement as he pointed to a set of footprints in the snow, a clear indication that Jimmy was well on his way to Culra. Retrieving some energy bars from his pack, Robbie handed them around.

"I read somewhere, best taken wi' water," Doc inspected the label while taking a quick draught from his CamelBak.

"What about whisky?" Donald offered his hipflask; Doc paused and studied the label.

"Doesnae say."

"Does it say *not* to?"

"Nope."

"Well then?"

"Aye… fair enough," He sipped quickly from the hip flask and handed it to me.

"Actually," I thoughtfully chewed, my mouth full of whisky and oats, "No' too bad; could be a market for that!"

"Ocht well it has succeeded in greasing the shoot," Donald fumbled in his pack for a roll of toilet paper and headed, like a man on a mission, behind a large rock.

Unwilling to be party to Donald's absolutions, we continued quickly down the glen, now bathed in weak winter sunshine as the last few clouds dissipated.

Robbie broke the contented silence. "Here Doc are things really that bad with you n' Susie or was that just the whisky talking?"

He glanced quickly over his shoulder at me, no doubt recalling our conversation, then returned his gaze resolutely to the path. "Acht so-so, it comes and goes Robbie, mostly it just goes."

Robbie waited patiently to see if Doc would elaborate, but he said no more. "Well things are no' so great for me 'n all boys, seems to be heading downhill fast with Sarah and eh... I've sort of met someone else," his voice trailed off and he marched silently on.

"*Whit?* You *are* shitting me, no way, fer fuck sake Robbie, well what eh... are you going ti do?" Doc glanced quickly at me, his usual dark scowl replaced by a look of surprise.

Robbie sniffed and took a deep breath, "Sometimes I think fuck it, one life why spend it miserable. Then other times I look at the wee fella and think why should I fuck it up for him? Fer shit what a mess, well, what are *you* going to do Doc?"

"Acht ah dunno Robbie, tough it out, keep myself happy by shaking hands wi' the unemployed. Eh... Scully here suggested I should take up golf!"

"Acht Scully, yah happy bam what do you know about being married eh...?" .

"Enough no' to do it!" I quickly retorted.

"Fer fucksake, Doc! Donald is happy isn't he, cannae be that hard?"

"It's no' the same thing Robbie, anyway ask Doughboy he'll just give you some Highland shite about sticking wi' the sheep the Lord chose."

"Aww c'mon, he's no' that bad."

"Aye he *is!*"

"Aye, well, have to admit I've avoided sharing *my* current dilemma!"

"What a pair!"

"Fuck off, Scully!"

"Aye well," Robbie sighed, "see this other lass, well it's just more fun."

"Grass!" Doc retorted flatly.

"Aye, always greener."

"You know maybe we should go out more regularly, blow off a bit of steam; you could be my wingman. Plenty of women out there for a good-looking bloke and his old baldy mate. Eh... don't mean to exclude you, Scully, but it might no' be easy for you ti get back for weekends."

"Nae bother!"

"Aye..." Robbie hesitated, "Well I'm always up for a night out and a few beers."

"Aye, if this lass has got any pals with a white stick and a dog, Doc here will be all set," I added provocatively.

"Get ti fuck Scully! Anyway, good stuff, Robbie, this sounds like a plan, so here has this lass you met got any friends, eh? Wi'out a white stick or a dog?" Doc rubbed his hands together gleefully, a sly expression on his face. "We could have some fun. I'm the perfect excuse for you, Robbie, and Susie is past caring where the fuck I've gotten ti."

"Eh... well I'm no'..."

"Look Robbie, we could take the van or head down ti Newcastle for a long weekend. I'm sure you can come up wi' a good excuse." Doc grinned lecherously, I watched Robbie closely, fascinated, waiting to see if Doc's blatant manipulation would work.

"You n' me Robbie wi' a few beers and a couple of babes sounds like an excellent idea for a weekend, and besides, Sarah wouldnae care."

Robbie stopped abruptly and turned, a questioning frown on his face. "Eh... what, why do you say Sarah wouldnae care?"

"Fuck eh...no reason..." Doc shrugged as he lied, the question of whether Robbie knew about the supposed infidelity seemed to have been answered.

At that moment, Donald swung into view and Doc mumbled, "Oh fuck, here's Doughboy; shall we change topic?"

Robbie made no reply and resumed walking, quickly putting distance between us. We waited for Donald and as we watched silently he strode down the path and off into the seemingly endless sweep of wild, untamable land that stretched to the glittering surface of Loch Ericht.

An hour later, we stopped once again, this time where the path crossed a small stream. Over the millennia, the flow of water had cut a deep gully into the hill, and the path curved into this invagination, disappearing from view before re-appearing again.

Donald stepped off the path and began to take a piss. Just then we heard a low rumble in the distance and turned quickly to look for the fighter jet. The RAF frequently traversed these glens on low-flying exercises, on route to their bombing range off the West Coast of Scotland. Robbie soon spotted the plane and pointed at the small, black, darting shape. It tracked along Loch Ericht at about five hundred feet, just below the snowline, almost hidden against the mottled backdrop.

As the jet banked slightly and headed north towards Rannoch Moor, we watched its progress, noting the disconnect between the grey-black shape and the distant roar of its engines.

Then, at precisely the moment I turned to Doc and commented, "They usually travel in pairs!" the second fighter jet banked over the bealach between Ben Alder and Beinn Bheoil.

It screamed right above us, the black shadow seemed to darken the sky, instinctively we flinched and ducked. A split second later, the deafening scream from the engines followed. I could almost feel the heat from the afterburners.

"Fer Fuck...!" Doc yelled, as we scrambled in shock, reacting even though the danger was over. Five hundred feet above us in the almost clear blue sky, the pilot already banked the multi-million pound aircraft. In those few seconds he'd covered the length of the glen, swerving sharply to the left to avoid the massive bulk of Gael Cairn. In seconds the shadow was gone behind Beinn a Chumhainn down the glen, and across Loch Ossian. As we stood and caught our breath the reverberating roar from the engines echoed and gradually receded.

Meanwhile, Donald had noted the first Harrier as it progressed along Loch Ericht and crossed Rannoch moor. The second jet, however, had come right over his shoulder as he stood urinating into the long grass. He was so startled that he pissed all over his hand and his leg.

"Feckin'... fuck!" he screamed at the departing shadow. Angrily, he inspected the growing wet patch that stretched rapidly down his leg. In the eerie silence now followed. All Donald could hear was the receding sound of a jet engine and us, breathlessly laughing our heads off.

As we turned and headed back to the Bothy, Donald trudged behind shouting loudly about Feckin' Biggles and maintaining that an independent Scotland would not let the RAF do this type of shit

Then on we tromped along the path. Biggles was soon forgotten as the subject changed to the plans for our second night, Burns Night.

Back at the Bothy, after a statutory cup of whisky-laced tea, Robbie and Donald headed out to retrieve the two bundles of wood. When they returned four pairs of hands made short work, and by the time the sun had sunk below the tree-clad ridge the cut wood had been stacked by the fireplace. Warmed by the exertions of sawing and stacking, we sat outside in the fading light, enjoying salty Cup-a-Soups.

Donald flipped the pages of the Bothy book. "Ocht well, jakey Jimmy left no entry."

"No' sure he *could* write and fuck him anyway he was low level would have seen nothing

"Aye here's to Banjo for providing the impetus to get us off our arses and back here, he would have loved that today." I felt a sudden tinge of sadness as I made the statement and the reality of how totally true it was hit me.

"Aye, you know I realised up on the hill today, why it was Doc here had spoken so enthusiastically about this place. At the time I just thought it was pint number four or maybe five."

"Ocht probably an equal contribution from both!"

Robbie swept an arm towards the distant hills, "To be fair this is a pretty magical place I mean the atmosphere the location, the total isolation."

"Aye fer fuck… missing yer phone?"

"Naw actually you know what I've no'."

"Yah lying shite, you were checking it up on the Ben!" I shouted.

"Ocht here, whit the feck Robbie, this is the place to recharge, and revive." Donald winced as he stood up and felt his aching legs, "Feck, I was going to propose a toast!"

"Better have a wee dram of the rejuvenation juice first, then!"

"*Finally* one of you is talking sense!" Doc threw the last of his soup in the tall grass held out his cup and shouted, "Aye, ready!"

After the bottle had been passed around Donald raised his cup, "Now then, here's to us; wha's like us?"

"Aye damn few and they're a' deed!" I finished off the well-known Scottish toast and got an appreciative nod from Donald.

"Aye to Banjo, *and* to all our other absent friends!"

"Gone but never forgotten!"

We responded with a unanimous 'Aye,' ceremoniously lifted our cups and drained the contents.

After one last lingering glance at the rapidly darkening sky, indication that the endless conveyor belt that is the jetstream was bringing something colder and wetter, we gathered our stuff and headed in to light the fire. As we made our way silently back into the Bothy, we each placed a gloved hand gently on the brass plaque.

10 THE TIN CAN

It was perhaps no coincidence that Banjo with his noted resemblance to the 18th century poet had originally suggested we should have a 'Burns Night' celebration at the Bothy. Among Robert *'Rabbie'* Burns many fine works are sonnets extolling the virtues of haggis and whisky and tradition dictates that on the anniversary of his birth both are consumed and his poetry recited. It has been argued. By the ill informed, that haggis is virtually inedible if not washed down with whisky, explaining the enduring coupling of the two. Perhaps for some but one thing was as true in Burns Day as it is now. Like most things in life, you get what you pay for, and cheap whisky will not wash down a cheap haggis. As the poetry was of the very highest quality then so should be the whisky and the haggis, so McSweens and at least an 18-year-old it was, nothing less.

Robbie switched on his head torch, inspected his plate and looked enthusiastically around the room. "Right then who's going to address the haggis then?"

There was silent anticipation as we gazed at our laden plates. Donald opened his mouth as if to recite the opening stanzas of the Burns poem but Doc cut him off, "Ah fuck it, we're four days late, let's eat…"

Clearly no one felt much like arguing with Doc's customary succinct appraisal and following the ceremonious opening of four cans of McEwans Export, silence fell upon the room. Ravenously we shoveled the food into our mouths, stopping only to breath or to wash it down with gulps of malty Export. Robbie finished first belched, grabbed a handful of dry-roasted peanuts threw them in his mouth and chewed intently.

"Here, how many calories do you reckon you've had today then, young Robbie?" My stomach felt fit to burst and I was very, very impressed by the continued consumption.

"Pffffew," Robbie considered my question thoughtfully his cheeks stuffed with half-masticated peanuts. "Well, eh… I'm no' done YET but probably someplace over four K at the moment."

"Aye fuck we probably all are," Doc agreed, holding his plate up to his face and scraping the last of the food directly into his mouth.

"Ocht, what, here, wait a minute! is this a Weight Watchers meeting or something?" Donald's voice had a tone of incredulity.

"Reasonable question…"

"Aye, for women!" Donald cut me off sharply.

"You have to consider these things, Doughboy old chap, see this is exactly why you're such a fat fucker!"

"Fuck aye!" Doc laughed clearly delighted at Donald's irate expression.

"Ocht now you can feck off, you skinny bastard! But here," Donald turned and pointed accusingly at Doc, "You are no' that slim yourself, from what I can see you've got a bit of a beer gut on you!"

"Well Doughboy that's 'cause every time my wife goes on top and pounds my belly flat yer wife comes by and uses the big pink straw ti blow it back up again."

"Ocht aye, well, that explains your fat arse then! She must be blowing too hard."

"Get ti fuck!" Doc growled then turned on Robbie who was grinning with delight. "Aye, you'll soon put on the pounds young pup, your sexercise days I'll be over. Just wait until she gi'es you the Santa suit!"

"Yeh what eh, Santa suit?"

"Aye… cause like him you'll only get ti come once a year."

"Ocht now leave the laddie alone, here Scully, talking of the overweight, you worked in America, what about those fat bastards?" Donald asked with a cheeky grin.

"Aye, what are you referring to the land of opportunity Doughboy?"

"How is that?" he shouted his face irate his voice shrill and indignant.

"Well see now, Doughboy," I responded dryly, "In what other country on the planet would Michele Bachmann, Sara Palin, or Rick Perry seriously be considered for anything more demanding than running a tombola stand?"

Doc roared out a hearty laugh, "Aye well, perhaps but still better then living back in the USSR?"

"Here it's no' like you to quote the Beatles, Doc!"

"Aye but Doc," My voice was suddenly earnest, "That's true, but just you try saying "Fuck" on the TV back in the land of opportunity see how far it gets you!"

"Ocht don't see a career in US TV in *your* future Doc!"

"Aye," I continued stifling a laugh at Doc's face, "And you cannae show Janet Jackson's nipple: a nipple, fer fuck sake, on the TV. Ho… but you *can* put on endless adverts with some bloke with a Hollywood drawl twittering on about, if you have an erection that lasts for more than four hours, seek medical advice!"

"Ocht aye," Donald smiled, "priapism the gift that just keeps on giving!"

"Aye well, perhaps it is all fucked up but then I'll take a fucked up system over totalitarianism any day!"

"And the ability to whine about it wi'out getting yer arse kicked, or worse, aye fuck it, Scully's yer right, it ain't perfect and they could certainly do more to tone it down in Westminster. But it's still way better than what most of the world get shafted wi'!"

"Ocht... here, now wait a minute!" Donald pounded his fist on his knee, his face glowing with anger. "That's still not a reason to settle for second best, it needs to be improved; you could do better! You'll see, an independent Scotland will be run properly, by the people *for* the people!"

"Aye Doughboy, life, liberty and the pursuit of a penis, as it were," I sniggered, as Donald glowered at me but Doc had turned to him.

"Aye here, you're off yer head; wasn't the final act of the last government we had in Scotland to sell its soul for English gold?"

"Aye, but that was *then*, this time around it will be better run!" Donald stabbed a finger for emphasis.

"*That is fuckin' shite*, Doughboy, obviously yer view is obscured because you've got yer fat ginger head shoved well up yer arse!"

"Ocht fuck you Doc!"

"Aye, *no way*, look you cannae trust them even if they set out wi' good intentions as soon as they can they're lining their pockets, selling out the ejits who put them there. Just shifting the power to Holyrood from Westminster will do fuck all, they'll bring their evil little habits wi' them!"

"Ocht no, there *will* be more accountability," Donald shouted earnestly as Robbie nodded in agreement.

"Aye yer barking, you'll no' change fuck all I'll tell you," Doc jabbed his finger in the air. "All you need ti know about democracy was put inti print in '45; all animals are equal, but some animals are more equal than others."

"Aye aye" Donald grabbed a bottle and thrust it at Doc, "No animal shall drink alcohol to excess!"

"Fuckin' A!"

We paused for breath, faces flushed with the excitement of the argument, then Donald took a breath and pointedly asked, "Ocht here, now how long before you get religion anyway, Scully, is that not mandatory in the USA?"

"Ah fuck of yah wee fat arsehole!" I was totally unimpressed by his transparent attempt to annoy me.

"Oh here, talking of religion, eh... we met Pube on the train, he's a ticket collector."

"Eh...?" Doc looked confused, he glanced sharply from Robbie to Donald and back again, "Who the fuck is Pube?"

"Ocht now, it was this lad who went to school with Robbie. Apparently, he used to have a beautiful head of curly hair. The stress and strain from the merciless taunting of a crowd of playground bullies teasing him about lice and crabs and calling him Pube resulted in the whole lot falling out and then, he found *God*!"

"What, was he in the *hair*?" Doc rubbed his own bald pate.

"Ocht now I'm not sure, did you ever ask him Robbie?"

"No, no I didnae, you bunch are fuckin' ridiculous at times do you know that? Now, more tea anyone?"

"Aye, here any chance of digging out a wee chocolate bar for dessert?" I added with a sly glance, "Donald here needs the calories, don't yah, Buddha?"

"Ocht aye, I believe I do, you great big scrawny streak of piss!"

The prospect of tea and chocolate and the need to sort out cups and dishes had the desired effect, heavyweight political and religious discourse was shelved for the time being.

Donald took a tentative sip from his tea added another generous dash of whisky and announced, "Ocht now… changing the subject from politics, I heard a funny story about Banjo a wee while back from Glen…"

"Eh… Glen?"

"Glen Lomshie, used to work with George, you know that big fat tosser, massive gut and white hair; lived in the bookies when he wasn't in Ryries. Ocht, here now Scully, was it not our man Banjo who gave George the nickname 'Skidmark?'" Donald laughed as he asked the question, which elicited a quizzical look from Robbie and a nod of acknowledgement from Doc.

"Aye indeed," I grinned broadly, "I believe Banjo labelled him thus, because he hung around making the place look shitty; you know, like a big skidmark in a toilet bowl and well, we all took turns trying to piss him off."

"Oh nice one quality moniker."

"Aye well, Glen was well out of the business deal wi' that arsehole, eh, he's working wi' Pete Holmes these days. I bumped inti him recently in Ryries, told him what we were coming here to do for Banjo."

"Ocht aye Doc and here did he tell you about the time he did a remodel job with Banjo on a posh house out Balerno way."

Doc stretched out his legs folded his arms across his chest and grinned wickedly, "Naw but you know what, I think I might have heard this one fi the man himself!"

"Ocht now Doc, it may not have been one he would have shared widely."

"Aww c'mon then, put me out my misery!"

"Well now Robbie, the tale as I heard it involved a home owner who was a real prat, gave them a hard time, asking why they're doing it this way or that and wouldn't it be cheaper and so on. It was driving them nuts."

"Nightmare!"

"Ocht aye well, by the end of the week they'd had a belly full, so they're straight down the pub for a dram and a pint and a wee while later things were looking much brighter."

In response to this snippet, the smattering of eager nods and looks of agreement, all indicated that for us at least such a panacea to a bad day at work was both widely used and eagerly employed.

"So now, a few hours on and a gallon or so of IPA later Glen suggested they call it a night. Of course seasoned bevvy merchant that Banjo was he picked up a nice wee ruby from that Indian at Haymarket, eh... the Verandah."

"Oh a splendid shop, excellent curries in there," Robbie smacked his lips.

"Aye true, here, I just had a mental image of Banjo doing the old vertical weave whilst emptying his pockets of assorted shrapnel and asking for a Tscchicken Maderass with extra flied rice."

"Ocht aye, probably not far off the mark. So... the next day, last day on this job, Glen said Banjo turned up looking a wee bit worse for wear announcing that he has been shitting the brown water but he had taken some anti-D's. Glen had to take off to get supplies, so he left Banjo mixing up a big bunch of plaster. He came back an hour later to find Banjo with a big tin can stuck to his arse!"

"WHIT how the fu...?" Robbie laughed with delight.

"Aye well now apparently no sooner had Glen left than Banjo had felt a deep rumble in his guts, clearly time to open the bomb bay doors; course there was no way he was taking a dump in this guy's house."

"IPA and spicy curry always a recipe for arse-blaster," I grinned exceptionally pleased with myself for thinking up this newly morphed word.

"Fer fuck sake..." Doc shook his head at me and sighed.

Donald continued, "Ocht anyway, he'd apparently struggled to the van doing the duck walk with his buttocks firmly clenched and noticed a big tin can of some kind of floor product; it was empty as well. So, he dropped his kegs and balanced it on the wheel arch."

"Oh hey sounds like luxury," Robbie nodded out the Bothy window currently being lashed with rain and sleet.

"Aye," Doc snorted, "you should carry in an empty can next year instead of all those full ones!"

"Ah... fuck off!" Robbie gave the middle finger to Donald, who grinned like an evil Cheshire cat.

"Now, when he let fly, it was just an enormous fart, feck all else, so he figured the anti-D's had put a cork in it. But it was at that point that he discovered that the can was firmly stuck on his arse!"

"Fer fuck sake, what was in the bloody can?"

"Some sort of glue for laminate counters or something, was all Glen said. Anyway… he got him to the A&E and he gives his details to a grinning nurse, all he could hear were folks sniggering loudly and even some bastard softly whistling the 'Cancan'!"

"Ohh, haha… people can be so cruel!"

"Ocht aye, so when the nurses did finally come and take him in to remove the can, their eyes are red they'd been crying and laughing so hard. Glen said when he got him safely back home Banjo got cracked into self - medication with a handy fifteen-year-old to sort out the pain."

"Aye that would do it," murmured Doc as he grabbed the whisky, "Just the trick!"

Robbie was chuckling and wiping a tear of laughter from the corner of his eye, "And tell me how long did it take for the skin to grow back on his arse and hee-haws?"

"Ocht well it does do exactly what it says on the tin."

"Aye… indeed," I kicked on my boots and reached for my down jacket.

Robbie stood up somewhat unsteadily.

"Oh aye jolly good, follow me young fellow we appeared to have synchronized bladders!"

"Aye take some penicillin for that."

"Jeez Doc, that's quite witty." I managed just the right amount of sarcasm in my retort as I snatched the cigarette that he had just lit from his grasp.

"Oi here fuck off!" he growled.

Outside a gap in the clouds rewarded us with a transient glimpse of a stunningly star-filled sky. Standing in the lee of the Bothy, we switched off our head torches and gazed up at the light show.

"Superb eh?"

"Oh aye, amazing truly amazing!"

"How many years before you can bring the wee fella along on a trip like this then Robbie?"

"Hah, no' sure Sarah would have that, she'd worry about what bad habits he might pick up!"

"Aye true, very true I'd no' bring Angie, the stories she might learn, she'd maybe have second thoughts."

I smiled as I thought of Angie dropping me off at the airport, waving me off on my six thousand mile round trip to meet a bunch of guys and places who were just a set of images on a phone screen to her.

"Aye, bet we could tell her a thing or two about you Scully!"

"Aye there's been some good tales tonight we're all on fine form, that superb day out has helped the mood. You always know its been a grand day and we're in for a good night when even Doc starts to wax lyrical, though to be fair the subject matter is one dear to us all."

"Aye, it's funny I eh… well I maybe saw a different side of him, you know. That's no' to say that any of your tales of his antics surprised me, he told me enough himself for me to know that!"

"Aye well we're all mellower Robbie, except maybe Doc but then he summed it up, cannae stay a daft wee laddie for ever. We'll raise a glass or in this case a plastic cup and fondly remember the whole man, even if we focus on just the good and maybe a wee bit of the bad!" We both had a chuckle at that. "Anyway here, as far my antics go… well I reckon Angie probably knows it all by now, though truth be told she's maybe had a wee bit of a sanitised version."

"Aye that's the one Sarah gets an' all, mind you she's seen me in action, so she probably fills in the blanks."

"Aye, it wouldnae take much imagination, but here I seem to recall she's a bit of a party animal herself, I remember her that time at eh, Glastonbury, wasnae bothered by the rain and mud just wanted to knock a few back and get you up to dance. Aye that was a good year, only two days of rain, we'd a ball did we no'!"

"Aye that was it, so here do you get out much in Boston?"

"Oh aye, couple of good places some no' bad gigs, we have a blast, Angie is up for a night out at least once a week or so an' that's all I can manage at my age," I chuckled a little self-consciously, "What about you two?"

"Ah no' so much, what with the wee fella need to get a sitter, it's no' so easy so we dinnae go out together much these days."

"Aye… how can you no' get a sitter, are there no' a few bored teenagers hanging around trying to earn a few quid for their next bevvy or bag of glue?"

"Aye that's part of the problem Sarah never liked the look of any of the local kids, wouldnae trust them with wee precious." Robbie sighed, and dug his hands into his pockets.

Taking a final drag on my cigarette, I flicked it in a glowing arc into the river, which swiftly swept it away. As I turned and headed back to the Bothy I gently admonished, "that's nae good Robbie, that's nae fuckin' good at all, she's a keeper that one, a lovely lass and you make a great pair, no' sure you should be giving up on that one my friend."

I left the comment hanging in the air as Robbie stared thoughtfully at the starry sky. He shivered dug his hands deeper into his pockets and turned and quickly followed me back to the Bothy.

Suddenly he stopped, "Oh here check it out Scully, looks like we're in for company."

I backtracked quickly, looked up the hill and soon saw the distinctive flash, "aye, your right Robbie solo hiker!"

We walked to the edge of the Bothy and watched carefully as the light moved slowly clearly headed downwards. I raised my head so the light from my torch shone towards them and moved my hand once across the light. After a moment of hesitation, the light turned towards us and emitted a single flash of response.

"Brrrr," I shivered, "They've a way to go! We'll put the kettle on in half an hour!"

11 THE V-WEE

Donald greeted the news of a visitor by noting, "Ocht here, could be Jimmy coming back?"

"Nacht that jakey bastard doesnae have the baws!"

"Aye well looks like they're on the path, I flashed them and they flashed back, single flash though so no need to go rescue whoever it is, I reckon they'll be half an hour maybe more."

"Ocht well, we should maybe go out and guide them in, they'll not see the candle from that side!"

Right on cue the wind rattled the window and howled down the chimney.

"Fuck that we'll need another nip before we head out!" Doc grabbed a bottle and passed it around. "Nae rush right Scully?"

"Oh, half an hour, at least, no rush." I shuddered as I looked out the window and quickly passed the bottle to Robbie.

"So here Doc, you getting the VW back out on the road for the summer? I might jump the pond again for that!"

The VW or V-Wee, as it had been known for many years had once been Banjo's pride and joy. A '74 VW camper in a two-tone livery of blue and white bought years before from a 'man in a pub.' A frustrated Banjo had sold it to Doc after a litany of mechanical problem had severely tested his budget and patience. After a winter of mechanical rehab, Doc had it back on the road puttering like it had just rolled off the line, sporting a Rolling Stones logo on the side door.

"Ocht that smelly old thing," grumbled Donald, "I tell you Mhari used to complain about the smell of petrol coming off me for days after I'd been in that!"

"Fer fuck sake, that's the smell of freedom, Doughboy!"

"Freedom? Here have you old codgers heard of the environment?" Robbie chuckled.

"Fuck off, anyway aye she'll be out the lockup in April I'll have her tuned up in no time, the hills are calling,"

Doc paused and frowned thoughtfully while I happily reminisced and recalled the distinctive 'putt putt' of the V-Wee's air cooled engine.

"Here eh… Scullo, what was the name of that lassie who came along wi' Banjo when we went up ti climb the Liathach that year?"

"Oh fuck," I grimaced, "Eh… Jane err…Wilson aye Jane Wilson."

Doc chuckled an evil throaty laugh, "Aye that was her, here do you think they kept in touch?"

"Here eh what's all this about then? Robbie's curiosity was piqued,

Stock stifled a laugh, "well, we were all in the Cask and Barrel and we got talking about hill walking and what great times we'd had. Anyways, this lass Jane seemed keen on going hiking or maybe she just wanted ti spend more time wi' Banjo. So, Scully here suggested a weekend away in the van, heading up North. We'd all had a few beers so it seemed like a great idea and next weekend we're on the road, forecast looked great, couple of cases of beer, some wine and party pack or two of midge repellent! So anyway first night out we stopped behind the Kingshouse eh… after we'd eaten and had a beer or two, Banjo and Jane disappear out ti his tent, course in no time at all, all you can hear is giggling and whatnot. I happen ti glance out the window and somehow, Banjo had managed ti kick out a pole so one end has collapsed. I'm treated, if indeed that is the right word, ti the sight of the perfect outline of his arse pumping away merrily! Aye I will never forget the sound of a sweaty arse rubbing against wet nylon,"

Doc shuddered and tried to look offended.

"So we certainly wernae inti watching or listening ti that, so to the bar eh, pronto Tonto! Next day we'd an early start and a cracking hike up the Buachaille Etive Mor."

I nodded vigorously in complete agreement, The Great Shepherd of the moor, to give it its English name, was always one of our favorite hikes and it had been a perfect day for scrambling up a mountain.

Doc continued, "when we got down off the hill we'd a couple of well - deserved cold ones in the afternoon sun, then jumped straight in the van and headed north up ti the wild lands of Torridon. Of course that's about a three hour drive wi' Banjo sat in the back wi' Jane and a fridge full of beer! So, by the time we pull of the road at Loch Torridon, sun was setting and he was feeling no pain, totally liquid so he was and Jane, she was fast asleep."

"Aye she was a bit of a lightweight for a Banjo burd."

"Aye, well we finish the day off wi' a wander, well in some cases a stagger up the road to the Ben Damph, nice wee boozer! Now next day we'd another fuckin' cracker of a walk along the ridge of the Liathach, absolutely stunning! Fuck me tell you what Robbie but that is one big bad boy of a hill! What a day out that was glorious sunshine tromping back down the glen ti the welcome sight of the van and…"

"The fridge!"

"Aye indeed Scully, an' after a well-earned ice-cold beer we drove back ti the campsite, on our way we passed that terrible camp-site, the one with the high hedge."

"Oh here I've been to that one, totally useless meant to keep down the see breeze I suspect but just provides a windbreak for the local midges!"

"Aye…" Donald voice took on an ominous tone, "and not just any midges Robbie, those are Achnasheen midges!"

"Fuck aye," I chimed in, "mind the time we climbed Slioch, Donald? No' a breath of wind and hazy warm conditions, the wee bastards were relentless. Every time we stopped, they fell on us in a feeding frenzy. They didnae relent until well over two thousand feet and they were just as bad on the way down, straight to the nearest bar after that hike. Eh…next day the ache in my legs had a distinct sense of *déjà vu*, reminiscent of the Peruvian marching dust incident."

"Aye wee bastards, anyway back ti *my* story." Doc brought our less than fond reminiscing to a halt. "We headed back ti the free camping site. Next thing we know Germans, Spaniards and an Irish couple had deserted the other campsite and joined us seekin' shelter fi the midges. Later on, we've settled down on the sand dunes under an amazingly starry sky with a welcome blaze. The midges had gone to bed or whatever," Doc paused and frowned thoughtfully, "You know that van has some kind of magnetic attraction or maybe it was the fire who knows, in no time half the campsite was gathered around. They're bringing over more beer and wood and it's turning inti party central."

"Pulling out the guitars and banging out a few tunes might have helped as much as any magnetic attraction of the van you know!"

"Fuck aye," Doc readily agreed, "Some pretty good tunes got banged out that night. Anyway, as Scully mentioned Jane was a bit of a lightweight and at some ridiculously early stage of the night she crawled off and crashed out in the van. Now Banjo and Scully here began entertaining two of the German girls who were decidedly NOT normal!"

"Eh…!" I cried out, instantly offended, "You, are you kidding, not normal? No way, that Katja was smoking hot!"

"Fer fuck Scully, they were laughing at yer jokes," Doc offered pointedly. "Anyway," he raised a hand to silence my protests. "At some point Banjo and one of the German lasses wander off ti get more wood.

They'd been gone a while when Jane only wakes up, gets her second wind and re-appears ti join the party. So 'course she asks Scully where Banjo is and he tells her he's gone for more wood. So off she traipses, I believe she found him behind a sand dune?"

Doc paused raised an eyebrow and looked at me.

"Aye, I readily agreed, "As I recall in flagrante, going decidedly balls deep inti said Fraulein!" Then I quipped to a predictable chorus of groans, "So eh… a woody was involved!"

"Aye right, well, next day, boy talk about a frosty ride home, if looks could kill Banjo would've been a dead man!"

"Awkward…" I added in a comically high-pitched voice, "She was pretty pissed off wasnae even in the mood for rebound sex!"

"Aye seemed ti remember that didnae stop you fi' trying Scully. Anyway trip home we took turns sitting in the back wi' Jane who had a stinkeye on the back of Banjo's head; she had a face on her like a bulldog licking piss off a wasp's arse."

"Aye, she bailed out a Fort Bill, demanded to get the train back."

"So, did you think Banjo ever heard from her again, then?" Robbie questioned with a half smirk on his lips.

"Naw, nor Katja for that matter!"

Suddenly, Donald brought the cheery topic to an abrupt end as he pointed out the window and said, "Ocht head torch!"

"Fuck," I looked at the window, " that was quick!"

12 RUPERT AND ELIZABETH

The nerve-jarring squeak of the outside door confirmed an arrival, followed by muffled voices and the sound of chairs being moved in the other room. Quizzical glances were exchanged and Doc stood up to boil water for more tea.

"Well I only saw one light but sounds like more than one!"

"Ocht here, not very friendly now, are they?" Donald offered an opinion on our unmet guests.

"Fuck naw they're just getting their shit together." Doc sat back down again, strategically facing the door. Minutes later, it swung slowly open to reveal a young man in his twenties. He looked cold, his lips almost blue.

Robbie was closest to the door, "Come in, come in get yourself by the fire."

"Oh I say, thank you," the visitor responded in a clipped English accent, then moved forward to reveal his companion, a girl also in her early twenties. Her head was covered in a white woolen hat, strands of brown hair framed her face. She was an archetypal 'English Rose', with alabaster white skin, blue eyes and ruby red lips. She shivered and hugged herself.

"Pretty cold through there," offered Donald.

"Yes, yes," the young man moved closer, holding his palms out towards the heat. "We came from Culra Bothy; we couldn't see this place until we were a few hundred feet from it," He looked like he was going to add to this but stopped himself. "We could smell the smoke from your fire, though!"

"Did you no' see us signaling?" Robbie looked incredulous and glanced at me. "I could have sworn one of you flashed your light back, that's why we didn't come to look for you!"

"Oh yes of course, sorry, thank you for that…" The young man frowned and looked at the woman, who said nothing.

"Ocht well, good thing you could smell us long before you saw us, anyway come in warm yerself!" Donald jumped up vacating a seat.

"Oh, really, are you sure? That *is* very decent of you."

"Ocht yes, of course, it's a Bothy after all, its not as if it's ours."

At this invitation, the girl moved closer to the fire and crouched down, held her hands to the flame and shivered. Doc gave Donald a sideward quizzical glance and lifted up the bottle of whisky. He grinned slyly at me as he nodded first at Donald then the bottle to indicate an inverse relationship between such hospitality and the level of the amber nectar.

"Well, thank you, that's splendid," The young man paused and removed his hat to reveal a shock of curly brown hair. He brushed off the coating of snow and ice and quickly put the hat back on.

"Oh I am terribly sorry, I am forgetting my manners, um... I'm Rupert and this," he looked at the girl and paused but she just stared at the flames as if too numb from cold to realize why he had stopped, so he continued, "...Is Elizabeth."

"Oh, but my friends call me Liz," she suddenly exclaimed, her face lightening up as she smiled.

"I'm Scully."

"Donald."

"Robbie."

There was a short pause, Rupert waited patiently.

"My friends call me Doc but you, *you* can call me Craig."

"Ocht," Donald snorted and shook his head in reproach, "just ignore him, grumpy wee shite."

"Aye well he actually prefers to be known as wee fat Doughboy!"

"Feck off Doc!"

"Ah well good, well, it is terribly nice to meet you, all of you!"

"So ahh... you came over from Culra?"

"Yes, we headed up over this afternoon, to the bealach."

Rupert said the word 'bealach' very precisely, Elizabeth nodded in mute agreement and shivered.

"Here, would you like a drink It'll warm you up?" Robbie thrust the whisky bottle and a plastic cup towards her.

"Well... thank you," she grabbed the cup with both hands.

Nodding at Rupert, Robbie thrust out another plastic cup.

Rupert grasped the cup and examined the peaty colored liquid, "Oh, is there any water?"

"Ye dinnae mix something that's been nestling in an oak barrel for eighteen years wi' somat that fell out the sky yesterday!" growled Doc, his eyes flashed but stayed firmly on the fire.

"Ah yes well, this will do, as it is then!"

"Just ignore that," I laughed and pointed an accusing finger at Doc, "he throws it in his tea!"

Rupert was suddenly aware that four pairs of eyes were looking at him. Donald held up his own cup, "Slainte?"

"Ah yes indeed," he followed Donald's lead, taking a large sip.

"So where yea fi?" demanded Doc.

"I'm sorry?" Rupert frowned at the colloquialism.

"Where are you from?" Doc repeated slowly.

"Oh um…London," replied Rupert, "Kent actually."

"You fi London an all," Doc addressed Elizabeth.

"Somerset, Taunton."

"We're both at St Andrews, and in the University Mountaineering club." Rupert scanned the room proudly as he announced this.

A short silence followed as we digested the information, Rupert and Liz belonged to a group of people whom we would usually have little time for. Wealthy Southerners, judging by their duck down jackets and expensive boots, who beat a path to St Andrews because after four years of education. What they would know was nowhere near as important as who they would know. Strangers perhaps, and from a world we knew nothing about but we'd welcome them regardless because the Bothy was still a sanctuary for all, and besides, Liz was a very pretty girl.

"So I say, are you guys in some sort of club or society then?" Rupert turned his head swiftly in response to the derisive snort from Doc.

"Ocht no," Donald replied, "Eh… there's a group of us we used to come here at the same time every year, hadn't done it for a while."

"Ah… there are four other guys with us, but more experienced climbers; they are staying at Culra and doing a few routes on the Northern face."

"Culra you say, ocht, now they will have some fine company tonight," Donald laughed.

"I'm sorry, why do you say that?"

"Ah well we had a guest last night he was very, very obnoxious and he disliked a number of ethnic groups with a passion. Now, are they all English, your friends?"

"Yes they're Yorkshire lads, all big chaps though!"

"Really," I grinned, "Four climbers two ice axes each per chance?"

"Ocht now, you know Scully, there are times when you just want to be a fly on a wall in another Bothy." Donald happily shook his head no doubt to a picture of Jimmy being chased by burley axe-wielding Yorkshiremen.

"Well he'll no' be sharing his whisky."

"I'm sorry?"

"Oh never mind, long story," Doc growled as Rupert and Elizabeth just looked nonplussed.

I changed the subject, "It was ideal conditions for climbing today."

"Indeed," Rupert nodded thoughtfully, then pointed at the laden shelf and asked, "I say do you guys always bring so much whisky?"

"We bring enough," Doc growled menacingly without taking his eyes off the fire, "An' it's the good stuff!"

"Ocht here now, what's your plan for tomorrow?" Donald's voice was softer and less menacing as he shook his head, irritated by Doc's aggressive tone.

"Uh… not sure, what about you?"

"Ocht, we'll decide in the morning when we see what the weather is thinking of doing."

Suddenly I had an idea, "here, if you dropped your packs at the bealach, you could nip up to the summit of Ben Alder then back down and on out to Culra. But it's a long slog: You'd need to get a very early start."

"Yes thank you uh… Scully," Rupert sipped his whisky and looked thoughtfully at Elizabeth.

"Aye," I continued enthusiastically, "be less boring than just retracing yer route, mind you I don't think it will be as nice a day as today, in all the years we've been coming here we've rarely seen conditions like that!"

"Oh and do you guys always base yourselves here?"

"Ocht yes this is a nicer Bothy than Culra, more remote but with access to wood." Donald gesticulated at the fire.

"Well we'd heard this was nice, I was actually struggling a bit slowing down poor Rupert here but then we met a terribly nice chap who told us we should definitely come here." Elizabeth's eyes were now looking a little brighter the warmth and the whisky appeared to be having an effect.

"Nice chap, you say? Well, couldnae have been that jakey Jimmy."

"Coming *down,* you say?" I frowned quizzically, mentally calculating how we had not encountered him.

"Yes, late afternoon, why?"

"Oh nothing, we were on the top at about noon, didnae see anyone but we headed down the back way; got here late afternoon. It's funny but in the past when we came here we would rarely see anyone else, I guess the word has got out!" I winked at Robbie who nodded enthusiastically.

"Well you may meet him yet; he was a very fit-looking chap. He informed us that his intention was to climb Beinn Bheoil, then either come here or traverse down and head for Culra."

"Ocht really?" Donald looked impressed, "Now that is some hike, both Bens in one day and in winter!"

"Well that's what he told us!" Rupert looked at Elizabeth; she nodded.

"Ocht well, there is plenty space here if he makes it!"

"Well, we are terribly sorry for the intrusion, but he said we would really like it here," Elizabeth smiled sweetly at Donald.

"Acht Liz, it's a *Bothy*, all are welcome," he grinned in return and thrust out the whisky bottle.

"No' all!" Doc added softly

"Here, it's my first time here too a bit chilly and basic, but the whisky helps keep you warm!"

"Basic? Here now, we have luxury soft furnishings this year," Donald thumped the Chesterfield, "We never had *this* last time we came here!"

"So, why the hiatus?" Rupert looked first a Donald then back to me and pointedly ignored the snort of disdain from Doc.

"Ocht, well, as I said we eh…" Donald scratched his chin, "We eh… used to come here regularly, then few years back our mate John, known to all as Banjo, was killed in a bike crash." He sighed softly, "now see, he was also kind of the organizer-in-chief when we did come. In fact, it was his idea to start coming here in the winter in the first place. So eh… we didn't go that year, then I moved over to Arran and Scully here got a job in the States."

I puffed out my cheeks and sighed. No one else spoke.

"Oh that is *so* sad," Liz gushed with charming sincerity.

"He wouldnae have wanted us ti stop," Doc mumbled and stared morosely into his cup.

"Was he married… your friend?"

"Banjo, no, but he had eh… has a sister, lovely lass called Maggie. Anyway, Doc here met her one day last year, and she told him what he'd had put in his will. Eh, that his ashes should be scattered on Ben Alder. So as we always came in at this time of year it seemed appropriate. And it would seem the mountain gods smiled on us, because that was a perfect day we had today!"

"Ocht now still organising us in a way, isn't he?"

The mood suddenly seemed lighter, the reminder of the cracking day we just had on the Ben had clearly helped.

"We also put a plaque up by the front door."

"I noticed that, the brass one, it looks very new, it's a lovely gesture, did… Maggie not want to come?"

"Ocht no, she's not really the outdoor sort, well certainly not outdoors in winter, we have said we will try to bring her back in the summer!"

"Scully the scientist, reckons there will be a patch of greener grass where we scattered him!"

"Oh … what is your employment in America … Scully?"

"I'm in Biotech."

"What made you join the diaspora?"

"Eh…" I shrugged I was trying hard not to laugh, I could imagine Doc thinking 'Stuck in a fuckin' Bothy wi two ejits using fancy words!' and the contorted dark dance that his face was performing was testament to this. "Ah... it was work mainly I did the usual: Went to London then kept going. I reckon I'd never have left if I'd have landed a job like Donalds!"

"Oh, really? And what is it you do, ah ... Donald?"

"Me, I work in a distillery," Donald carefully placed the whisky bottle on the floor, stood, groaned loudly and headed for the door. When he returned a few minutes later he announced, "Ocht here, it's a rotten night out there the rain is back on now, reminds me of the night you and Banjo had your eh... bike crash!"

I shuddered involuntarily at the memory.

"I say Bike crash?" Elizabeth's face morphed into a look of concern, "What, were you with er... Banjo?"

"Yes but this was an earlier scrape," I reassured her, "A few years back. We've actually all given up the motorbikes these days, except Donald here, but even then he only rides his on Arran."

"Ocht, got to watch out for sheep; that's the main danger, these days!"

"Aye, or catch them and take them back to your man cave," Robbie quipped as Elizabeth looked confused at the strange tangent the conversation had taken, but before she could ask for clarification, I resumed telling the tale.

"Anyway, I dinnae remember how exactly but we'd managed to get hold of a new tire on the cheap. I was giving Banjo a lift home, so er... there might have been a few beers involved. Now, he got it into his head that it was a good idea to sling the spare tire bandolier-like and sit on the pillion seat of the bike. Actually, his arse was almost hanging off: there's no' that much room on the back of a Triumph. So, we're jamming it down Broughton Street in the pissing rain and just as we hit the roundabout, a taxi appears from nowhere. I had to swerve or we'd have been toast and I lost the back end course the bike starts fishtailing." I motioned with my hand to indicate a wild swerve, "and Banjo fell off!"

Elizabeth let out a slight gasp and looked at me open-mouthed.

"Aye, well I got a handle on it, but thanks to his tire bandolier, Banjo was off and rolling. He took a couple of wild bounces and ended up stuck to the top of a wrought iron fence, hanging head down about fifteen feet up in the air!"

Both our guests now wore looks of extreme confusion, so Donald weighed in, "Are you familiar with the New Town area of Edinburgh, at all?"

"Actually no," replied Rupert. Elizabeth shook her head.

"Well now, it's full of Georgian terraced houses that have basement flats, probably for the servants. So, the main door to the house has a set of steps leading up to it, and a second set leads down to the lower basement level. Then there's a big wrought iron fence with ornate spikes between the pavement and the drop."

Rupert and Elizabeth nodded, now able to understand Banjo's predicament.

"Aye," I continued my tale, "One spike was through the tire and into his old leather bike jacket."

"The one with the tassels on the sleeves that some lassie dumped a bottle of patchouli oil over?"

"Aye that was the one, Robbie, that thing was seriously minging so it was; Banjo could clear a room with the smell from that. Anyway, there he was, he'd bounced and kind of half gone over this rail with a spike through the tire and a second spike stuck through the back pocket of his jeans into well, into arse. Meanwhile, I had recovered control but it was only for a fraction of a second then I lost it again on the wet road. I ended up putting the bike down and rolling a fair way down the road myself."

"Were *you* alright?"

"Aye, I was fine, few scuffs and a bit of road rash. I limped back up the road, and together with the taxi driver we tried to pull Banjo back up, but of course the spike was into his arse a wee bit."

"How terrible, whatever did you do?" Rupert blurted.

"Waited for the fire brigade; they winched him up after the longest twenty-two minutes of his life!"

"What a pair!" Donald, shook his head with a disapproving look.

"Well, perhaps you should have taken a bus if you'd been drinking that much," Rupert admonished.

"He didnae know how ti drive a bus!" Doc growled.

"My god, you were very lucky," Elizabeth added.

"Aye, I'll drink to that," I cut her off and raised my arm, cup aloft and added somberly, "Here now, to absent friends!"

"Aye," the others agreed.

"Banjo needed a few stitches and a tetanus jag, and the tire was toast but all in all..." During the thoughtful silence that followed I changed the subject, "When was the last time you had your bike out, Donald?"

"Ocht I only use that in the summer, ice and bikes, not a good idea!"

"Hey, did you ever get a woolen seat cover?" Robbie grinned cheekily.

"Ocht feck off, you yah wee..."

"I'm sorry, but what is it with all the wool and sheep jokes?" The confused look had spread back over Rupert's face.

"Ocht well now see," Donald let out an exaggerated sigh, "These soft Southern types maintain that we tougher Highland boys, well we need the help of the local livestock when it comes to satisfying our err... urges."

"Did you know?" Doc turned to Rupert, "That when Doughboy here lost his virginity, the lucky girl's mother was there!"

"Good god, man," Rupert blurted, a look of shock on his face, "How on earth did…?"

Doc cut him off, "aye, all she could say was Baaaaaaaa."

As Elizabeth shrieked and laughed, Rupert just looked decidedly uncomfortable and not in the least bit amused.

The effects of the whisky, the tall tales and the warmth of the fire seemed to have finally lifted Elizabeth's spirits as quickly as it lowered any inhibitions.

"So tell me is it true, *is* this Bothy haunted?"

The question had an immediate effect, as Donald who willingly warmed to the task of telling ghost stories.

"Ocht now, ghosts these hills are full of ghosts, you can hear them howling all the time, but this place, McCook's Bothy is definitely haunted!" He said the word 'definitely' very slowly and precisely. "See, old man McCook lived here for many years with his wife and the ponies. This was in the Victorian era and in the summer, the rich folks from the lodge would get a boat up here to Ben Alder Bay. Now, part of McCook's job was to know where the stags would be feeding, and then get his guests to a point where they could get a decent kill shot. He'd done this for many a year, but then one winter Mrs. McCook fell ill and had to be taken out to Dalwhinnie. Sadly there she died, so that was him left all on his own."

"Aww, how terribly sad!" Elizabeth sounded sincere.

"Aye well, he managed about another five years. That's five long cold winters with the gales and snow and as you've seen, there's not exactly a lot of creature comforts here! Anyway, one year a particularly bad storm kept the resupply boat from making it down the loch. When they finally arrived, they found him in the porch between the two sets of the doors." Donald turned and pointed at the door with a comically trembling finger, "Hanging there, dead!

Doc snorted loudly in derision but Donald persevered, "Best they could tell the isolation just got to him, and he couldn't stand it any more, since that day the Bothy has been haunted, by old man McCook. Sometimes you hear footsteps other times he's dragging furniture around in the other room, and…" Donald concluded with an ominous tremor in his voice. "When it's a full moon, the worn out part of that front step fills up with blood."

Rupert's mouth moved as if to query this but before he could, Doc cut in. "Absolute total and complete *shite*!"

A grinning Donald sipped his tea and nonchalantly shrugged his shoulders.

"Ocht well, now, actually there was a book called err… 'Undiscovered

Scotland' written by some bloke called Murray back in the Fifties. I believe it details a run-in with McCook's Ghost."

"Aye, it's all complete nonsense," Doc spat dismissively with a withering sneer, "He died peacefully in his bed in Newtonmore sometime in the Thirties. The story about this place being haunted was started ti keep poachers away. If you read the rest of that chapter the only thing he does find here, is a bunch of lads who'd been poaching deer."

"Ocht no" Donald cut him off, "There's a long bit in that book about them being in here and hearing furniture moving in the other room and that," He waved a hand in the direction of the corridor as he grinned at Rupert, "Is why we always kip in here, quieter see."

"We kip in here cause there a fuckin stove. I'll gi'e you this much, there are plenty of tales in there," Doc nodded curtly at the Bothy book. "Folks wi' overactive imaginations or no doubt after way too much whisky, hearing all sorts during the night. Clog-dancing mice most likely; there's no' been any sightings of Old Man McCook since he was alive; he's probably hiding out someplace wi the Loch Ness Monster and Mo fuckin' Johnson!"

"Ocht well then," Donald suggested calmly, "Perhaps it's not Old Man McCook that haunts the Bothy, but that French boy then, the unknown man."

"French Boy?" Robbie scanned his face for a telltale smirk that might suggest this was a tall tale.

"Ocht aye, it was a few years back now, We must have been up on the hill when the corpse was there. We actually came past the site of his demise today.

"Ocht aye," Donald smiled, he loved the myths and legends of Scotland, and in particular the ones surrounding Ben Alder Bothy. These he collected these and recalled them with enthusiasm.

"Now, they reckoned it was suicide, but as usual the conspiracy boys had other ideas. He was found over on the flank of the Ben facing Carn Dearg a single bullet in the chest. He had removed all the labels on his clothes, had on a rubbish pair of shoes and was not in the sort of gear for being out here at anytime of the year. As I recall that they had to reconstruct his face, and by chance a friend of the family was in Scotland and saw the poster or some such."

"And I say what did the conspiracy theorist have to say?"

"Eh… that it was an assassination, there was supposedly money involved. He'd traveled all the way from France, then found a remote and isolated spot and topped himself; guess he didn't want to be found. But I reckon his ghost is probably still wandering the hills to this very day."

"Total shite," snorted Doc.

There was a brief silence as we considered this latest story, then Elizabeth asked with a cheeky grin. "I say so can you sometimes hear him running past the window howling 'Oui!' or is that just the wind?"

Donald stared, somewhat taken aback then Robbie broke the silence, threw back his head and roared with laughter. "Oh that is *awful* Liz, that is the kind of rotten pun I've come to associate with Scully!"

Elizabeth looked very pleased, her face flushed and glowing, if Donald's intention had been to try and scare our guests with his ghost stories; it didn't seem to be working. He persisted though, holding up his hand and coughing lightly, when he spoke, his voice was hushed and full of gravitas.

"Ocht well now way back in 1951, five guys actually died doing exactly the same walk that we completed today," he nodded at Robbie.

Robbie looked shocked, "You never told me about *that* before we started!"

"Ocht aye, it was during a particularly bad December storm; they tried to make it over here to the safety of the Bothy, but got beaten back by the weather. When they finally opted to turn back and tried to retrace their steps to Corrour they'd left it too late. One by one the party succumbed to the weather. Only one of them struggled through and tried to muster a rescue party. Back in the Fifties though, such things were not well organized and when they did come back it was all too little and way too late."

"Fuck, me that is hardcore!" Robbie's eyes were as wide open as his mouth.

"Ocht five more ghosts wandering these cold windswept hills," Donald intoned, his voice comically ominous, "You know, it might just have been their gear and the winter weather, but more than likely it was just sheer bad luck."

"Aye, you can get bad luck crossing the street in Embra'; c'mon, shit happens, we've all got good Karma right," I thrust the whisky bottle at Rupert, who pretended not to notice.

"Here, aye there was also the crashed plane from during the War," Robbie, changed the subject slightly.

"Ocht aye those poor bastards…"

"What was this all about then?" asked Rupert.

"No' sure exactly but eh…" Robbie looked at Donald who nodded as if to carry on. "Eh… I was reading up on the place before I headed in, supposedly bits of an old plane near the top of Carn Dearg. The story goes that they were practicing bombing runs. Whatever they didnae make it, so…"

"Probably a few more ghosts for you there then, right Doc?"

"Acht, get ti fuck!"

"Well I suppose Banjo will have plenty of company here, then!" Elizabeth noted cheerfully.

Rupert looked sharply at her perhaps concerned that we might find the comment insensitive, but Donald cheerfully added. "Aye, indeed Liz, probably be one called Jimmy by the end of the night if he pisses off your mates from Yorkshire, now then eh... Tea, anyone?"

Doc reached for the whisky and held the bottle out, "Fuckin' ghosts," here, put some spirits in the tea, will you!"

"Oh... er, I say, not in mine thanks," Rupert paused as he became aware that all eyes in the room except Elizabeth were now looking at him. "I think I've actually had enough," he explained weakly.

Sporting an evil grin, Doc put his face close to Rupert's and growled, "Go on, go on or the terrorists have won!"

Snorting out a half shriek, half laugh Elizabeth covered her mouth as Rupert mumbled, "Well I suppose, a small one then, it does uh... actually seems to be warming me up!"

"Good man," responded Doc loudly splashing whisky into a cup before he staggered out the door. An accompanying cacophony of vibrating doors and stomping feet heralded his disappearance into the night. Several minutes passed before he reappeared and crashed noisily into the room.

"Here, Scully you're a scientist, maybe you know, why is piss yellow?" He slurred the question.

"Eh... cause if it was red you'd be shitting yourself," I replied with a nonchalantly.

13 TAM THE HAT

Silence fell upon the room; that strange hiatus when no one is all that sure where the conversation as such should go next. After several minutes pensively staring into the fire, Robbie roused himself. "Here, did you ever hear the strange tale of Tam the Hat?"

No one responded, though Donald gently shook his head.

Taking the silence as his cue Robbie began, "Well, this was back in the 70s, an era that fashion forgot, or maybe it was just having a very, very long laugh."

"Fuck aye," snorted Doc.

"Now, see Tam and his wife Kate had this wee bull terrier called Meg, pugnacious wee fucker so it was. It was giro day, see, so Tam has his dole money and he's off to the pub with his sidekick wee Johnnie Souter."

"Ocht here now, hang on a minute," Donald began to interrupt, but stopped when he noticed Robbie wore a broad grin. The characters he had heard mentioned at the start of his tale all had the same names as the main protagonists in the epic poem 'Tam O' Shanter' by Robert Burns.

"Well, we are supposed to be celebrating Burns Night, and we've no exactly overdone it with the recitals tonight so instead I thought I'd update a classic tale!"

"Aye now are you familiar with the poetry of Rabbie Burns?" I questioned Elizabeth and Rupert.

"Ah yes, some of his stuff," replied Rupert, his tone suggested uncertainty but then he noted. "Was it not, uh… last week?"

"Ocht yes, the 25th, but we couldn't get the time off, so we are having our Burns Night tonight."

"Ah, I see."

"Well I'm sure he wouldnae bother."

"Course no' he's fuckin dead!"

Robbie sighed, "aye thanks for that, Captain Obvious, anyway, see this particular poem was set sometime around 1790 and tells of a Scottish lad who drinks too much, ignores warnings from his wife and almost meets with an unfortunate demise at the hands of Auld Nick and his demonic horde."

"Right enough, not much change with modern Scottish lads then, eh!" Donald noted with a laugh as we sat back and listened, curious to hear how Robbie would deal with a modern day rendition of a classic tale.

After the statutory pause for liquid lubrication Robbie began to tell his tale.

"Well now see, one stormy night Tam announces that he's going out for a pint or two and of course Kate gets tore right into him. Reading him the riot act about his behavior, casting up the fact that he lost most of his last dole money on the horses. She'd also been told that he was out drinking last Sunday and had stayed out for hours and had been seen in the company of a wee slapper name of Jean who lived in Kirkton. Of course, he's no time for any of her nagging so he grabs the dog's leash and heads for the door, and out into the night.

"Now all he could hear is a tirade of abuse, along the lines of what a fuckin' drunkard and a waste of space he is and why doesn't he get a job. She keeps it up though even screaming out the window that if he keeps on drinking and behaving like this he'll end up dead in a ditch! 'Course Tam takes absolutely no heed of this and heads up the road. Having totally ignored her sage advice, in no time at all he's teamed up with his drinking buddy Johnnie Souter. Soon enough they're on a pub-crawl first stop the 'Grey Mares Tail', then into 'Drouthy Neighbours.' Now… once ensconced in there the beers are soon flowing freely." Robbie stopped briefly and glanced around, he need not have worried we were all still listening, enthralled.

"So, Tam finds a plum spot at the end of the bar next to the fire were he can regale the Barmaid. She pauses frequently to listen as first Tam then Johnnie tells one outrageous story after another. Of course, Tam is pouring on the charm as usual, whispering something dodgy in her ear, usually to an accompanying loud shriek and giggle! Meanwhile, outside a storm is brewing and the rain is coming down in rods. Several loud flashes and cracks of lightning are followed moments later by the low rumble of thunder. At one point Tam shouts 'Fer fuck sake's that's pretty evil weather out there, auld Nick must be about!', which elicits another shriek of laughter from the barmaid. Now, as it's a Friday night there's a DJ of sorts setting up the karaoke. Before you know it, Tam and Johnnie, encouraged by the barmaid have joined in the singing and frivolity and time, as it has a habit of doing on nights like these, flies easily by. Before long, Tam has had a skin full. He's actually got well beyond the point of caring about just how pissed off Kate might be. Meanwhile outside, the storm – clearly angered by the oblivious devil-may-care attitude of the drunken pair – shows absolutely no sign of easing off."

Robbie paused and sighed dramatically. "Ah, well my friends, as we all know, oh all to well. All good nights must come to an end as time waits for no man. So Tam finishes his beer and bodes Johnnie farewell, grabs Meg's leash, shrugs on his jacket and heads for the door. When he steps outside, thunder n' lightning are crashing across the night sky, the wind is howling like a fuckin' banshee and the street is totally deserted. Pulling up his collar, he sets off at a fair clip hands dug deep in his pockets, hat pulled right down quietly whistling a merry tune to himself. He splashes off through puddles illuminated orange by the streetlights, each filled with a thousand dancing raindrops. Now, in no time at all he's back on the Old Dalkeith Road and walking past Newington Cemetery, bent double into the howling wind. But just at that moment, he notices lights flashing far off in the distance and just then, the rain seems to case off a wee bit. The wind drops enough that in the distance he thinks he can hear music. Well now, maybe he was emboldened by the whisky, who knows but for whatever reason, curiosity gets the better of him. So, pushing open the old iron gates he headed towards the light. For some reason, the ever loyal and pugnacious wee Meg was actually straining at the leash wanting to go in the other direction. But Tam was curious and bold, so grabbing the leash a bit tighter he urges her on. He figures maybe it's a rave or something but he's up for it so he heads closer, cautious but very inquisitive."

Robbie paused again and looked around the room but we were all sat staring into the fire listening intently

"Now… he gets to within about thirty feet and stops dead in his tracks slowly taking in the scene. There's a really gnarly looking dude, long hair all fucked up looking with like a sheep's skull on his head. He is giving it big licks on a fiddle but its scratchy no' really in tune. Gradually, as Tam's eyes adjust to the dim light, he realises that some of the graves are open and the coffins are upright and stood ajar. There are folk apparently dressed up as the dead, dancing around holding lights and there is a lot of weird shit lying about on all the gravestones. Blood, gore and other accoutrements of violent crime: bloodstained Buckfast bottles, knives, daggers, and the like. Then… the gnarly looking dude really starts to up the tempo and the dancers start to get into it. Some are going hard enough that they've begun to shed their clothes. Of course for his part Tam is a bit out of it so all this registers, but it doesn't really sink in, he's just standing there mouth gaping like a goldfish totally mesmerised by this Bacchanalian scene. Just when he thinks this shit couldn't get any weirder, a young girl in a flowing white dress gets up and starts to dance to the scratchy fiddle music. Now Tam watches, absolutely transfixed, as she swirls and pirouettes. Her hair and the flowing dress becoming a blur as the thunder rolls again and the lightening flashes. She just whirls, dips, and weaves, all flowing white and peroxide blonde. The evil-looking dude with the goat's head is really pounding out the tunes and it's actually the best bit of dancing Tam has ever fuckin' seen. Then suddenly he just forgets how weird this all is and how dodgy they all look and he cries out!"

Robbie suddenly jumped to his feet as if to emulate Tam's actions, he held up a clenched fist and shouted. "Get on yerself yah beauty!" Then he quickly sat back down and dropped his voice to a whisper. "Now, at this interruption the lights somehow just go out and Tam is stood there frozen, riveted to the spot, trying to figure out what the fuck just went on. Meanwhile, Meg suddenly starts howling and straining at the leash pulling Tam in the opposite direction. At first, he doesn't move but then another flash of lightening, reveals a horrific sight. The entire horde is rushing towards him and they don't look happy. Tam catches the glint of a variety of broken Buckfast bottles and blades flashing in the light and that's all he needs, he's off like a bat out of hell. Heading towards Cameron Toll Shopping Centre, a quick glance over his shoulder and all he can see is the fiendish horde close on his heels. Over a wall across a road and a final desperate herculean effort of a sprint. He even briefly manages to get ahead of Meg. She'd needed no encouragement and was running as fast as her wee short terrier legs would carry her. Then, *then*, just at that moment, that crucial moment when all seemed lost, Tam could actually feel the demonic breath on the back of his neck! Kate's parting comment about him ending up dead in a ditch ringing in his ears. They got to the small bridge that crossed over the burn at the back of the shopping centre. Meg suddenly lets out a half howl half yelp followed by a total unnerving silence. As for Tam, well, he barely slowed down, merely glancing quickly over his shoulder to see where Meg was. But, as he paused, he realised that the horde had stopped on the other side of the bridge. It soon became clear that they wernae either willing or able to cross. Tam was of course, exhausted so he stopped hands on knees gasping for breath his chest heaving, carefully watching the evil horde. They in turn just milled about on the bridge in the dim light of a single lamp. Someone, or *something* was preventing them from advancing. Tam couldnae see what but it was clear they wernae moving any closer. 'Fuck you yah radge cunts' he finally shouted breathlessly while flipping a finger at them but that was as brave as he was willing to be; they were still freaking him out. He swiftly turned and hurried on home, Meg trotting dutifully along next to him. Now... as soon as he got home, Meg took to her bed, a reproachful look on her face as if to say 'What kind of shit did you get me into this time yah f'in ejit?' Tam, well, he didnae notice this reproach as he'd already rushed to the kitchen and got a can of beer from the fridge, headed straight for his front room and with shaking hands, skinned up a fat and totally loaded joint before quickly smoking it. Of course, he couldnae sit still and got up a numerous times to check out the window but he needn't have worried the street was deserted there was no sign of the 'weird bastards' he'd just seen. After mulling it over, he finally concluded that someone maybe Johnnie had slipped something in his last pint. A bad batch of 'E' perhaps or some acid, the whole thing had just been a bad trip. So then, he turned to silently fuming, enraged that anyone could pull such a cheap fuckin' trick on him. Finally, he took to his bed quietly running through a mental picture of everyone who had been in the bar that night, his mind racing as he tried to figure out who had slipped what in his beer and why."

Robbie paused and grinned at the rapt expressions of the assembled company then he concluded. "Now... the following morning Kate shaking him roughly woke him up and the conversation went something like this.

Tam, Tam....' it was Kate shouting in his ear.

What. he responded drowsily

What the fuck did you get up to last night yah bam?

Nothin'... I was out with Johnnie in the pub

Aye, she spat out the response, well what the fuck happened to the dog's *tail*?

Tam wearily raised his head and with bleary eyes looked at Meg, she was stood in the door wagging a short stump, her tail *was gone...*

Of course he just slumped back and covered his eyes recalling the previous nights strange goings on and silently mumbling to himself, that is *it* I am never going to drink again!"

Robbie surveyed the room; he wore a broad grin and looked decidedly like he was waiting for acknowledgement,

"Oh ho... nice one, aye, *like* it Robbie!" Donald clapped a hand on Robbie shoulder.

"Here, how the fuck did you come up wi' *that* then?"

"That was excellent, really excellent!" I enthused and smiled feeling elated, Robbie had done a great job with a classic tale, though Rupert and Elizabeth looked totally nonplussed.

Robbie was clearly enjoying the plaudits. "Aye, I've been thinking about that for a while; kinda modern twist on a classic tale," "I figured I would replace the horse with a dog but still have Old Nick and his entourage pursue them until reach the safety of the key-stone of a bridge, as the original tale suggests!"

"Brilliant, loved the karaoke, classy touch," I toasted Robbie with my whisky-filled tea. "You and your adaptions, Robbie first Binyon, now Burns; is there no end to your talent? Here, does make you think though," I added thoughtfully, "I mean if ghosts and boogles dare not cross running water as the original poem suggests. Well eh… Scotland is maybe no' the best country in the world for them ti live in!"

"Oh, I say is that true?" Rupert demanded.

"Aye, supposedly," Doc sneered dismissively, "but it's all just stories!"

"Well," I added, "You really have to have read the poem, but in the original Tam rides a horse and it's the horse that loses its tail, but no more, because the pursuing band of ghosts stop at the key-stone of the bridge, Robbie here just brought it up to date with a few modern touches."

"Yes, well," Rupert noted, "I'm sure it all makes sense…"

Smiling proudly still obviously pleased with himself Robbie grabbed a bag that hung from the wall and pulled out some cheese and a pack of tortilla wraps. He quickly slapped two of the wraps down on the hot metal of the stove top then used his knife to peel off thick chunks of cheese which he dropped onto the wraps. In minutes, the cheese began to melt and bubble, Robbie spread it out with the knife.

"Brilliant Govan Pizza, yah beauty!" Doc rubbed his hands gleefully and licked his lips.

The contrast between this and the appalled look on Rupert's face could not have been more extreme. I did not care, perhaps he was offended by the hygiene standards, Robbie's filthy hands the equally dirty stove or maybe he just did not like pizza. Elizabeth looked less appalled, more curious perhaps as she watched Robbie's cordon bleu masterpiece bubble and spit. However, she shook her head and laughed, when, like a gentleman, he offered her the first 'pizza'. Doc showed no such reticence as he grabbed the still bubbling offering and happily dug in. Robbie just continued peeling chunks of cheese onto more wraps. As I eagerly grabbed one and munched happily I reflected that it probably tasted a bit like a warm pizza box coated with cheese.

"Hey you sure you don't want one?"

"Ah I say it's terribly nice of you but… if we're to make an early start, I think we must go." With that, Rupert stood and stretched.

Elizabeth reluctantly finished her whisky, sighed and added, "Just as I was finally beginning to feeling warm as well!"

"Fuck, more for us!" Doc ignored our departing guests and shuffled slightly closer ready to grab the next cheesy creation before Donald could.

"We've got lots more whisky," Robbie grinned and held up a whisky bottle. At first, Elizabeth did not move while Rupert waited by the door poised motionless like the bottle of whisky. Then she slowly shook her head, swept the room with a broad smile and said, "Oh well, goodnight and thank you for making us feel so very much at home!"

"Aye, nae bother!"

Once more the old wooden doors creaked and slammed until the cacophony of noise gradually subsided and was replaced by the cheerful crackle of the fire.

"Poor thing, don't think she ever got warm; she still looked a bit blue."

"Aye, she needed more whisky."

"Or body warmth…"

"Fuck aye, some offer was there was room in yer bag Robbie!"

"Some slack in your sack perhaps?"

"Ocht for fu' would you two just not have to always, always lower the tone." Doc and I chuckled in mutual delight at Donald's irritation, which only caused him to glower even more.

"Fuck it, cheer up Doughboy, you had a chance to tell yer daft wee ghost stories, we'd have told you to shut-up if it had just been us."

"Oh Doc eh c'mon", I remonstrated, "Those stories are part of the Bothy and these surrounding hills!"

"Acht," he sneered and shook his head.

Donald looked slightly smug at my siding with him, "ocht here there was something a bit odd about them though wasn't there?"

"Like what?"

"They were just…"

"English!"

"Aye well there is that but I was thinking more of their lack of any whisky in these winter hills."

"Aye fuck, English and novices!"

"Well, here still no sign of the mystery hiker then, should we light another?" Robbie pointed at the candle on the window frame, it had flickered its last.

"Ocht aye, I'll get it, not that it will do much good as Rupert noted you can't see it if your coming off the Ben, if he's still out there now he's in for a cold night!"

"Aye," I shivered at the thought, "Hopefully safe and warm at Culra!"

"Fuck aye," Doc agreed, "even the prospect of a night being entertained by that we fuck jakey Jimmy would be better than a night hunkered down on the hill!"

14 PLAYER OF THE YEAR

"So, have you been into Ryries recently?" I addressed Doc.

"Aye just last week, I bumped inti that wee pest, Jimmy Black, I used ti share a flat wi' him. *Vomit*, ah will always associate the man wi' fuckin' vomit."

"How so, Doc?"

"Ha well see Robbie, Jimmie had an awfy habit of throwing up violently at the sight or sound of anyone else calling for Ralph or Hughie on the great white phone. I shared a flat wi' him and Banjo, what a pair for the bevy. Anyway one night I'm on the sofa watching Telly and I hear this scraping sound at the door, turns out it's Jimmie trying ti insert a fifty pence piece inti the keyhole while simultaneously attempting ti hold up an even drunker Banjo upright... I've no sooner let them in and got Banjo inti the front room when he throws up across himself and the carpet! Course Jimmie instantly takes on the appearance of eh... the bastard child of a hibernating hamster and a puffer fish. Ah head for the door ti find a bucket or towels but too late, fuckin' redecorated an entire wall so he did."

"Aye very nice, so did you warn the bar staff about his propensity for spewing forth or even a very close second in his case."

"Oh fer fuck," Doc groaned at my latest pun, "Here, now by the way, talking of Jimmy n' Ryries, what about Ryries Rovers, Scully, Doughboy remember them?"

"Aye of course how could we forget what a team, here you should have played for us and no Middy's Magyars what a bunch of tossers Robbie!"

The decidedly flowery name of this team was conceived in homage to Ferenc Puskas and the legendary Hungarian side of the 1950s. Robbie had joined them before we could recruit him and sadly we'd never played on the same field as Middleton's Magyars, despite their grandiose moniker, had been three divisions lower in the Edinburgh Amateur Sunday League.

"Aye, fuck, it's been a few years since we turned out in the black and white. Here what was that other lot oh aye, Mathers Marauders. Err… you played for them an all did you no', Scully?"

"Aye, I did until I started drinking in Ryries."

"What was that boys name we picked up from Mathers?"

"Other then Banjo the other one was eh… Ikea."

"Oh wait what, Ikea!" Robbie screeched the name, his voice filled with incredulity.

"Aye, well," I explained, "Ikea was so called because he was all class and style but completely non-functional with a tendency to fall apart under pressure or when wet! An appropriate moniker and on that topic do you know how Banjo got his nickname?"

"You know I don't think he ever told me, I was introduced to him as Banjo and after a while, well that's all anybody with the exception of his Ma ever called him, Bit like you Mr. Cully, course when I found out your first name was Steven it all made sense!"

"Aye, seem to recall it was 'cause my Ma' put 'S. Cully' labels on all my clothes! Anyway, Mr. Brown was a wee bit more contrived or at least less obvious. See we'd all started playing for Ryries and anytime during a game when he missed a good chance he would say 'Oh, fuck sorry ah… couldnae have hit a cow's arse with a…"

"…Banjo!" Doc and Donald happily completed the quote in perfect unison.

"Aye he also used to say he'd come a close second ti a one-legged man in an arse kicking competition."

"That's true Doc but that didnae lend itself so readily to a nickname, mind you I suppose we could've called him Cow's-Arse, but Banjo it was and that stuck."

"Aye fuck," Doc took a slug of whisky, "he was some player and a total nut case back in those days mind, he was a Postie back then and his route had a couple of hundred tenements on it. He'd have all these stairways and he'd just about do the equivalent of climbing Ben Nevis every day. Great guy to have in the team though… you know, slender one goal lead in the eighty-ninth minute so punt a long ball into the oppositions half. Who'd still have the legs to chase after it like a bat out of hell but…"

"Banjo!" I shouted and grinned happily at Donald.

"Ocht here, he used to get away with murder on and off the park."

"Oh aye, mind the Cup Final game against Roseburn United?"

"The one where he lined up against Psycho *and* got me sent off?"

"I seem to recall that wasn't your only red card of that OR ANY other season Doc."

"Fuck you Doughboy, bad referees scourge of ma fitba career!"

"Here whit happened anyway…?"

"Ocht well, Robbie, see, the game in question was one of the last times we all played together and it was surely one of Banjo's finest games. As Doc noted, he lined up against this boy who had the totally appropriate nickname of Psycho. Now, the relentless ongoing lip between the two was sandwiched between crunching tackles of the barely legal variety. Then, in the second half Banjo got a cross-field pass and he promptly nutmegs Psycho. Course this severely pisses off said nut job, Banjo's response predictably enough, was to nutmeg him again moments later. That alone was probably enough but as Banjo fired off a long ball and the play moved on he proudly noted that 'If he did that… one more time he'd get to stick Psycho on top of his tree at Christmas'. Course, Psycho got Banjo's wee dig, the suggestion that he had as much trouble keeping his legs closed as a Chrimbo tree fairy. So, next time Banjo got the ball, BOOM, tackle from behind and down he went like he was felled by a sniper's bullet. The alleged fairy then got a straight red."

"Aye," I chipped in to illustrate, "I'm pretty sure that had that tackle been on the street it would easily have resulted in an arrest for GBH."

"Ocht, very true, Scully but such a trifling detail didnae prevent Psycho from accusing Banjo of 'fuckin' faking it'. Eh… as I recall he suggested Psycho should save his breath as he'd need it to blow up his date later that night! Causing him to lunge at Banjo but he got no further than Doc here who promptly stiff-armed him, dropping him on the spot."

"Eh… actually it was an elbow then an uppercut, but it took him out right enough!"

"Aye now, it didn't help calm thing down much Doc! As I recall neither did Banjo's parting comment to a second adversary that he didn't half moan a lot but then so did the boys mother, when she was shagged up the arse!"

"Nice…"

"Aye now, when the dust or in this case mud had settled two players from the opposition and Doc here had been sent for an early bath. Still even without Doc's defensive skills…"

"Aye fuck, my motto was man or ball gets passed but *never* both!"

"Seem to recall most of the time it was neither!"

"Ocht, here now I always thought your motto was… one stomped into the ground the other sailing through the air!"

"Most of the time it was *both*!"

"Fuck off, you pair, it's a contact sport, no' dominos!"

"Aye, well, we went on to win that game easily with Banjo having a great game. The other team seemed a wee bit reluctant to tackle him, perhaps due to the referee's watchful eye."

"Aye," Doc took up the tale again, "After the game there was a stand-off in the car park. Psycho was snarling and swearing at Banjo. His parting comment was ti accuse him of having a fat arse. Banjo just grabs his crotch and said, "well you see you *need* a big hammer for a nail like this but then what would you know, digit-dick!"

"Ho ho… nice!"

"Aye," I added, "Seem to recall the Police finally showed up and escorted the referee no doubt straight to the nearest open bar. I'm sure he probably had a wee drink and some soul-searching consideration. No doubt around the relative merits of the financial reward he got for attempting to control such total debacles."

"Ocht aye here, couple of weeks after that we'd the player of the year awards and Banjo got the vote. No big deal right enough, ah mean there wasnae a fuckin' trophy or anything!"

"So it was just an excuse for the team to get together and have a bevvy then?"

"Eh, aye, aye, more or less, Robbie," Doc paused a thoughtful frown on his face as if the reality ingrained in this observation had hit him for the very first time. Then, with a quick dismissive shrug usually reserved for occasions on which no one had died, he asked, "Aye well, more tea?"

"Oh aye, ta!" was the unified response.

"I'll put the kettle on, on my way out," Doc announced, as he stood up stretched shoved on his boots and stomped noisily out the door.

As the night wore on, and more logs went on the fire, the room warmed and we chilled out and enjoyed the relative comfort of the Bothy. Something caught my eye as I stared into the fire. "That one looks like a dragon," I pointed at a burning log that was protruding from the flames.

"It's more like a shark!"

"Naw It's a dragon! Look, it's even got flames coming out of its mouth!"

"Ocht no it's a shark, look its got a wee bit sticking up like a dorsal fin!"

"Sharks dinnae breath fire!"

"Dragons don't have dorsal fins!"

"It's a *dragon*, here what do you say Doc?"

Doc peered in the general region indicated. "It looks like a burning stick, yah tubes," he declared and began to loudly sing, 'Ring of Fire.'

However, although he gave a passable imitation of Johnny Cash, he faltered briefly at the first chorus, stopped, and considered thoughtfully what if anything, to sing next. Then Robbie burst into song and proceeded to deliver a tuneful and a passable rendition of David Bowie's 'Drive-in Saturday'. We joined in enthusiastically *a cappella* with the accompanying chorus of 'Got got du aaah aah aah,'

"Excellent Robbie, very nicely sung,"

Doc passed round the whisky and suddenly blurted out, "Aye, good old Bowie," he paused and shook his head with a wry reminiscing smile, "Acht you know when I was a school there was this lass a couple of year older than me. Nicole was her name. Now, in addition ti being a raven-haired beauty of indescribable loveliness; she was also a big Bowie fan. She totally loved him and I in turn had her on a pedestal! Jeez, talk about unrequited and unattainable lust! Of course, it would have been social suicide for her ti go out with a lad two years younger. Just no' the done thing at school, so I lusted and I yearned until finally, crushed, I just moved on. Then a few years later I met her in a bar; still every bit as gorgeous, and oh, in a very... very... tasty wee black dress. So, I was turning on the old Doc charm, it was actually going pretty well, when suddenly, she turned and with a radiant smile asked, 'Here, you look kind of familiar, what school did you go to?'"

Doc spread his hands out and nodded sadly, "That, was it... the gig was up, my cover was blown. I had ti fess up and even admit the year, I want from smooth operator back ti plooky youth in one blink of those golden-brown eyes."

He sat still nodding sadly at the recollection of that night, a suitably reflective and poignant look upon his face then he added, "I tell you boys I swear they eyes o' hers were the same hue as a 17year old Balvenie double wood."

"Ocht, so no Bowie then eh... how about we sing something by the Stones *then* Doc, happier memories eh?"

"Aye... if you dinnae mind," Doc replied crisply, his poignant frown quickly replaced by a broad self-effacing yet evil grin.

There was a pause while we each pondered which Stones song, if any, to sing. To aid in the decision-making process I reached for the bottle and passed it around just as Doc lurched heartily into a passable rendition of 'Paint It Black'.

The night continued, and as the whisky flowed readily our faces became more flushed, our voices more strident the singing and frivolity louder and louder. We covered more of our favorites: Pink Floyd, Bob Dylan, The Beatles and Little Feat some were better than others both in terms of recall and tunefulness. The whisky-fuelled conversation lurched to new depths of ridiculousness and as the drink continued to flow; it headed even further spiraling out of control on its downward trajectory.

"Sho...." Doc slurred, " what's the stupidest question you've ever asked?"

"I once asked 'Do you think we should have one more for the road' when I was out *drinking* with you."

"Ocht I once asked the Mhari, 'How much did that cost?'"

"Aye, what about you young Robbie?"

There was no reply, Robbie had fallen asleep and now sat his head thrown back mouth wide open snoring softly.

"Man down," announced Doc, "someone update his Facebook status ti totally and completed fucked!"

"*Like* that, yah dobber."

Robbie's snoring began to get a bit louder, so I nudged him, which did succeed in silencing the noise. An unanticipated consequence was that he slid gently to the floor, curled into a fetal position and resumed his snoring. At this sight, Donald stood up, threw a sleeping bag on top of him and stacked their two therm-a-rests sleeping mats, spread out his sleeping bag and crawled in. He shuffled around grunting happily about 'effin comfort and 'effin luxury as he settled in.

Taking this as the cue for the end of this night, I climbed into my sleeping bag and went through the usual futility of plumping up my improvised pillow. Doc packed more logs on the fire, carefully shut the woodstove doors and climbed into his sleeping bag. Finally settled, he sat up, bag around his waist and lit a cigarette in the semi-darkness.

At the sound of the lighter, a mumbled, "Mnmm nm mnmnmm smoking indoors," drifted through a sleeping bag and two therm-a-rests.

"Ah fuck off, Bothy rules," Doc snarled then nodded at the prone figure of Robbie. "Here, Scully, we just goin' ti leave him there?"

"Robbie, yah ejit get in your bag!" There was no response, no movement, not a flicker. I considered the situation for a moment. "Aye fuck it, he'll be alright, 'sides I couldnae lift him if I was sober!"

"Aye yer right the big fucker will wake up when he gets cold and crawl off into his bag. Here, I tell you what, Scullo, that was some view today up on the hill; stunning, really stunning."

"Classic, absolute classic. Here, how may years, if ever before you see a sight like that, aye?"

"Oh aye it was superb; you'll only get a handful of those in a lifetime... *and* there was the added bonus of watching Doughboy piss on himself!"

"Fug Off," Donald muttered then rolled quickly over, "And you as well, Biggles, wherever the feck you are!"

A few moments later, Donald had joined Robbie in what appeared to be asynchronized snoring competition.

"Aye well there goes the backing band," I nodded at the prone figures, "so eh… my golf idea is a non-starter then?"

"Naw," Doc wriggled around in his sleeping bag as he sorted out an itch, he scratched himself briefly and settled back with a satisfied sigh.

"Here, maybe you should try therapy?"

"Eh…?" Doc looked askance, "whit the fuck are you on about Scully?"

"You n" Susie; you know, try to work it out, sort yourself out and stop your nefarious wee plan to lead Robbie astray."

"Ah fuck off Scully, this is no' America, it's Scotland, you can keep yer trick cyclists; besides, the depths of bitter resentment and hostility we have achieved is going ti be hard ti fix!"

"Oh c'mon, get on the couch, tell Doctor Feelgood about your childhood."

"Get ti fuck."

"Well, here, take the van, head off find yourself some happiness; you're all set, it's the perfect shagging wagon!"

"Aye indeed,' he sighed wistfully, "we'd some rare times in that van! Fer fuck sake Scully where did those days go? Life used ti be simple we'd have carried on fer ever smoking like a chimney, horsing back the whisky and eating a load of deep fried crap, and then died in our forties just like my Da'." Doc's voice trailed off into a frustrated silence.

"Acht," I was exasperated with his negative tack. "C'mon, I reckon you've time for one or two more rodes on the rideo, cowboy!"

He nodded slowly, "Right enough, way too soon ti jack it in. I've got ti do something interesting wi' my life, gie' you boys a story or two ti come ti the Bothy and tell about me!"

I just burst out laughing, really laughing. "Doc you've done more in a weekend than most folks will do in their whole lives. Story or two? Fuck, we're going to have to come in here for a week and bring a barrel when you pop yer clogs."

He laughed his evil wee laugh and looked smug, "Aye well, hah, perfect shagging wagon, aye right! Best get that Stones logo painted over wi' a big blue diamond these days. Here, we'd need a barrel for you an' all Scully!" Doc stretched his back and grunted, 'Tell you though, if either of us is wanting our ashes scattered here we better hurry up an pop 'em; no sure I've got too many more years of hauling this old carcass in here left!"

"Right enough, may have ti settle for a patch of grass next to the crematorium or the Meadows!"

"Pentlands would do, or even Arthur's Seat; great views fi both!"

"Fer fuck sake, Doc, you finally fallen for Embra's majestic skyline?"

Doc actually chuckled at that as I grinned and noted, "well, if you've got to spend eternity looking at something, eh…?"

"Here, have you made a will?"

"No, you?" I paused then with a comical look of fear asked "Eh…Why-

why d'ya ask?"

Doc snorted, "Your no' that high on my list o' folk I want ti kill."

"Gee, thanks!"

"Aye fuck, Susie's been on at me ti make one but I've no' that much ti leave; mind you, I better sort it out so the weans get it all."

I nodded silently; it seemed redundant to ask why Doc wouldn't want to leave his meagre fortune to his wife.

"Well, I'll take it as read that should anything happen to you at the theatre or on a drive through Dallas, you would request that I gather the troops and sally forth to the summit with your mortal coil in a suitable modified and empty Export can!"

"Eh aye fuck, more or less Scully; I'll do the same for you!"

"Aye, ta! Now you mention it, I probably ought to get a will together; no wanting the government to have my chattels! Maybe request a few tunes, see if I can get away with, 'Always Look On The Bright Side' as they slide me in, then again. Here… what about 'The Long and Winding Road' eh? There wouldnae be a dry eye in the house!"

"Ah fer fuck sake, Scully!" Doc cleared his throat irritably, "Now then, enough on this, think you can get a pass ti come back for a wee summer trip in the van?"

"Eh… no need I'd bring Angie, reckon she'd be up for that; wee holiday in Scotland an all."

"Aye… well," Doc sighed and it occurred to me that that was probably not the answer he was looking for. But then he just slid down into his bag and mumbled, "Goodnight then, John Boy!"

"Aye, goodnight, Mary Ellen," I replied as one of the logs on the fire exploded with a crack and showered the glass with chips of burning wood. I shifted my legs to ensure Robbie was not smoldering, then closed my eyes and almost instantly fell asleep.

It was probably about three hours later when loud snoring roused me from a shallow sleep. The room temperature had dropped precipitously and it was almost pitch dark, with all the candles having burned down and virtually no light coming from the fire. For a minute or two I was disorientated by the total darkness as I tried to determine where the snoring was coming from. I lifted my head from the stuff sack pillow, and quickly realised that the noise like someone sawing wood emanated from the floor and Robbie.

Suddenly, Doc made a quick movement; there was a brief pause followed by a dull thump as something heavy hit Robbie; he groaned softly and rolled over. The snoring swiftly stopped.

"Fer fuck sake," Doc muttered as the room again fell silent, save for the low moan of the wind and the slight creak of the ancient wooden panels as they moved and allowed its passage. As I again drifted quickly back to sleep, the images from the top of Ben Alder flitted happily through my mind's eye.

I woke again a few hours later with a sudden jolt; the fire had flared up and was blazing cheerfully. I could just make out a figure sat on the Chesterfield hunched over, hands outstretched head covered. I tried to raise my head but found I could not move. It was as if something was pushing down on me. In a half daze like a waking dream I relaxed as a feeling washed over me like I was falling but gently floating, softly, like a feather. Then as I drifted back to sleep. I managed to turn my head but the hooded figure just sat and stared into the fire; they did not return my gaze.

15 WEIRD DREAMS

I woke late; well late by Bothy standards, emerging slowly from the cocoon of my down-filled bag, I inspected the window with bloodshot eyes. Weak light filtered through the glass and illuminated the layer of frost and ice that had formed on the inside.

I eased out of the bag and fumbled for my boots. I found one, but was unable to locate the other. Confused, I switched on my head torch, scanned the room and located my boot and several others, all in the vicinity of Robbie's prone figure. I hopped over, pulled it on, grabbed my down jacket and stepped into the corridor.

The door to the other room was open. It was empty: Rupert and Elizabeth had gone.

The handle of the outside door was icy cold to the touch as I stepped out, squinting as my eyes adjusted to the dawn light. Several inches of fresh snow had fallen, and white horses danced across the surface of the loch as the wind blew in angry flurries. Nevertheless, it somehow seemed strangely peaceful devoid as it was of any of the claustrophobia of city life. In every direction mile upon mile of untouched snow coated the moors, mountains and forests. I stepped forward and began to whistle the opening lines of 'Splendid Isolation', as I pissed in the reedy grass.

The dawn chorus of flatulence was well under way when I returned and lit the burner. Behind me on the floor, Robbie was blearily contemplating the dawn; he shook his head and rubbed a newly formed bruise on his arm.

Doc pulled items from the hanging plastic larder, and a sizzling crackling noise with accompanying aroma soon filled the cold Bothy air.

After he had inspected his cup for whisky residue Robbie commented, "they're off already; must have taken Scully's advice and got an early start."

"Must have," I agreed, "I couldnae even see any footprints!"

"Ocht well it *is* snowing pretty heavily!" Donald bobbed up and down as he peered through the frosted up window.

"I never even heard them leave!"

"Me neither I was out for the count," Doc turned to Robbie, "some ejit snoring kept me awake for the first part of the night!"

"Aye, whisky sleep, you wouldnae have woken up with a blow job fi Angus!"

"Ocht here, whit the fu... a blow job from who?" Donald puffed out his cheeks and frowned.

"Aye, one of the first times we met and led young Robbie here astray, we took him along to a party and introduced him to eh... Remember young Agnes McVietch a-k-a Angus on account of her ability to give a blow job in the style of yon AC/DC front man?"

"Ocht, me I never had the pleasure."

"Aye she blew my hose and then she blew my mind."

"Very good Robbie, very good!" Doc nodded appreciatively at the twisted use of 'Rolling Stones' lyrics.

"Aye fuck," Robbie stared at the floor his eyes grew wide at a memory, then he smiled proudly and added, "Aye, she timed me, said I was in her top five for staying power."

"I think I was number one."

"Aye *right,* Scully, mind you," Robbie grinned, "when I came back into the party, I sat next to Banjo and noted what a gorgeous slim and petite figure she had. Do you know what he said?"

I nodded, "I believe he may have suggested that it was because *that...* was all she ever ate at the weekend!"

"Aye, that was it, Scully, fuckin' Banjo, priceless!"

"Ocht aye, well enough already. So here, maybe we should head up to the Annoch?" Donald took over and flipped the contents of the frying pan into the waiting pittas.

"Maybe we should go look for the fuckin' mystery hiker?"

"Well, whoever it was may have gone to Culra, isn't that what they said, eh... I actually thought the Annoch looked like a grand hike?"

"Aye, they did Robbie," I agreed then paused and contorted to scratch a bothersome itch with considerable relish. "But eh..."

"Aye well," Doc cut me off and frowned curiously one eyebrow arched quizzically as he observed my contorted scratching. "The Annoch is a fine hill but if this bloke fell or twisted an ankle, he's had a cold night or worse, we should head up the Bheoil."

"Aye could do," I grabbed a greasy offering thrust in my direction and briefly contemplated if Doc's sudden increase in civic mindedness had anything to do with finding a dead body.

"Aye well, fair enough, you make a good point; what say you Donald?"

"Ocht, we'll no see feck all either way, but if it closes in at least and we've headed for the Annoch, we can turn back, we'll still be in the glen."

"Well I'm heading up the Bheoil." Doc announced.

"Six of one half a dozen of t'other, the Bheoil is a grand climb."

"Aye," Robbie grabbed a pitta, "well me I'll go with the flow!"

Donald said nothing, he just stared out the window at the falling snow and nodded reluctantly.

Robbie took a bite and chewed thoughtfully on his breakfast, "You know ah had a *very* weird dream last night."

"Ah fer fuck, was that what was rubbing on my leg?"

"Aye," Robbie grinned, "ah woke up on the floor and there was someone sitting by the fire which was once again roaring nicely by the way."

"*Fuck...*" I blurted out in surprise. "I'm no sure that was a dream Robbie, see aye saw that n' all I woke up again just after Doc here had lobbed boot number two or three at you."

"Eh...whit?" Robbie rubbed his arm, scowled and bit into his breakfast. "Well who the fuck was it then?"

"I dunno see I couldnae raise ma head, I tried to sit up but it was like someone was pushing down on me!"

"Fuck aye, have you got a sore arse?"

"Oh shut up, Doc, no see I could see them but I couldnae move I was like eh... paralyzed or maybe eh... actually until right now I thought I'd been dreaming."

"Ocht well you could see *them* then, who was it?"

I frowned shook my and stared into my tea, "they had a jacket on and their head was covered by a hood!"

"Oh fer fuck sake..." Robbie's eyes grew wide, "That's what I saw n' all a hooded figure and I couldnae move *either!*"

There was silence, then a half sneer slowly appeared on Doc's frowning face as he spat, "*Aye...* so two drunk idiots have the same dream, think that's got anything ti do with the whisky?"

"Ocht well here eh... maybe it was the mystery hiker did anyone look to see if there's anybody in the wee room?" Donald pushed passed and opened the door, he returned moments later, "no empty, here maybe it was Rupert come through to get warm?"

Robbie snorted softly, "Naw... you know, I kinda thought..."

"Thought what?"

Robbie shook his head. "Acht nutin."

"No c'mon what Robbie?"

"Like I said I thought I was dreaming, but eh...I thought it was Banjo."

"Oh fer fuck sake, see?" Doc turned angrily to Donald, "That's what you get fi telling stupid fuckin ghost stories and drinking too much whisky, it probably was Rupert! come through here ti get warm!"

"It wasnae him, too big, what d' you say Scully?"

"Fuck I dunno… I thought I was dreaming but aye, acht, I dunno."

Donald stooped down again trying to see through the window, which had steamed up impenetrably almost as quickly as the ice had melted. He rubbed a small clear circle into one of the four panes of glass and thoughtfully considered the huge snowflakes now faintly visible as they swirled past the misted window.

"Ocht well anyway weird dreams aside it's not going to clear up any and it'll not be the same view as yesterday it's going to get worse maybe we should stay low level?"

"Aye what the fuck, if there is someone injured up on the hill we should go look, let's get going. Now then, you two done dreaming?" Doc sneered.

"Acht away ti fuck."

I shook my head and for the second time looked thoughtfully at Robbie trying to figure out what it was we had both seen.

16 SPARE MITTENS

The steep climb to the bealach was almost identical to the day before, but as conditions gradually worsened, any prospect of popping up through the clouds disappeared as fast as the wind-driven snow. We crossed to the right though knee-deep snow, the wind whipped at our backs as we made our way up a narrow ridge that stretched upwards towards the distant peak of Beinn Bheoil. Like ants on a birch log, our tiny figures edged upwards, the greens and blues of our jackets the only flashes of color in the vast expanse of black and white. Then, just as we reached the summit, the wind dropped as if it was pausing for breath, steeling itself for another onslaught.

The clouds lifted slightly and offered a view as a crumb for all that effort: a welcome crumb, nevertheless.

"Fuckin' great!"

"Oh here, this is some hill, I mean… the Annoch would have been great," Robbie nodded in the direction of Annoch Beag, " But this one, it's like when you see a gorgeous lass with her no' quite so good-looking mate. An you canny choose but you also just *know* deep down inside that the plainer lookin' one is going to be way mare fun then her high maintenance pal."

"Ocht here now what, are you on about, Robbie?"

"Eh… nutin, just eh... just blethering."

"Scully would just shag 'em both!" shouted Doc.

"Acht right Doc very droll, now lads, I'm not exactly the world's best tracker, but I've no' seen a single footprint in this snow," I waved a gloved hand, "Other than our own, the ridge is narrow: He didnae come this way!"

"Ocht aye whoever he was must have thought better of it and dropped down to Culra."

"Hopefully had a most entertaining night as four burly Yorkshire lads beat the living shit out of jakey Jimmy!" Doc rubbed his hands together gleefully at the thought of such entertainment. "Anyway we've done our civic duty haven't we? No sign of a body, so no point in hanging about, right?"

"Aye very true. So tell me, Doc, was it a corpse you were hoping for no' an injured man?"

He laughed and grinned almost sheepishly in a manner that suggested I had hit the nail square on the head.

"Aye well it's done n' dusted right enough, it's really closing in wind picking up, let's get ti fuck before it decides ti kick our arses."

We wasted no time and headed quickly down the hill into advancing clouds that swirled menacingly up to meet us. In seconds, everything was white, and visibility was down to two or three feet. Robbie was in the lead, Doc a few steps behind using his broad shoulders as a welcome windbreak. Heads down, ice axes at the ready, we scanned the ground ahead for our footsteps, trying to retrace them to safety. The wind screamed relentlessly in our ears as on we staggered doggedly like Friday night drunks, homeward bound on autopilot.

Even with goggles and my hood firmly fastened, the ice crystals whipped off the snow found a gap; like tiny missiles they lashed any exposed flesh. I trudged on, head bowed, almost blinded by the ferocious wind at times unable to see more than where to step next. When I did lift my head, I held my gloved hand inches from my face to deflect the icy projectiles.

In the distance, I could vaguely make out a dark shape, so I ducked back down, pulled my hood even tighter and tried to push on. The wind just seemed to increase its determination to blow me off my feet.

I stopped suddenly; some sixth sense told me this was not right: ahead of me loomed a large rock, the shape I had seen. I scanned the ground, looked left, then right, then turned and looked behind. I could not see any footprints. The muscles in my stomach tightened involuntarily.

Frantic, I scanned the ground all around me. Even though the visibility was only a few feet, one thing was clear: I was alone.

I turned slowly, then carefully and deliberately doubled back and scanned the ground for the vague indents in the icy snow. Another rock face loomed, and I crouched down and sheltered from the unrelenting wind. My heart pounded as I fumbled for map and compass, my fingers numb in the bulky mittens, like trying to play the piano in boxing gloves.

Suddenly, a gloved hand grabbed my shoulder.

"Ocht here now, where did you get to?" Donald's distinctive Highland lilt sounded calming against the scream of the wind. His whole face was covered by his hood his eyes hidden behind a pair of glacier glasses with leather side shields. He crouched down, loosened his hood and revealed his stubbly ginger chin.

"Dunno, thought I was behind Robbie… turned out it was a big rock!"

"Ocht aye I've noted the resemblance; I thought I was following you, kept going, then suddenly there were no footprints. Must have lost the trail way back amongst the scree. This is a bit wild though eh...?" Donald's face looked grim as he reached into his pocket and pulled out his GPS.

"Aye… so where are we then?" I nodded at the GPS, the screen flickered then went black. Donald slapped it several times against his hand and jabbed at the buttons but it remained dormant, its black screen devoid of life.

"Ocht *shite,* batteries must be dead."

"Well I just doubled back and you found me so… if we keep going in the same direction we might get back to the path, the one we came up on and then we can get ourselves off this hill." I folded the map and shoved it back into my breast pocket.

"Ocht for feck sake," Donald did not look in the least bit happy or convinced about this plan.

"How you doin'?"

"Feet are freezing but other than that, brand new."

"Right then," I tried to scrape off the ice that had built up on the Velcro clasps that held my hood, then covered up my face once more. At least the wind was behind us as we staggered on, treading carefully watching for our footprints, but it seemed angered by our persistence and screamed even louder blurring the snow and cloud into a total white out.

"Ahh… *fuck*!" I shouted, as I noted our tracks disappearing into the jumble of scree. Donald approached and we crouched down behind a boulder. I pulled out the map and compass.

"Right, here's the scree, so we are somewhere on the edge of this," I indicated the feature on the map and held the compass flat, but the needle floated aimlessly in circles, never quite coming to rest. "Must be these rocks. C'mon, let's move and try further on."

I raised my head, and scanned ahead fruitlessly. The visibility was still close to zero; on we stumbled blindly then we stopped again.

"Compass any better?" This time the needle held firm. "Sweet, right, let's head west;, I'll take a guess on altitude,"

I peered at the map over the top of my goggles. It flapped incessantly, making a noise reminiscent of that achieved when as children we had put old playing cards in the spokes of our bicycle wheels.

"Feck sake, Scully," Donald bit his lip nervously. He was not relishing the danger, or the uncomfortable feeling of his feet.

"Reckon we're here," I confidently jabbed at some contour lines and ignored the butterflies in my stomach. "See, we probably lost them amongst that scree, then we veered off, blown off-course by that wind, which we now have to walk straight into. Looks like some pretty steep ground further ahead."

"You sure?"

"Aye!"

"We could be here," Donald jabbed at an even more dangerous looking section of the map.

I wiped my nose with the back of my gloved hand. "Naw, I think we're here; we need to go that a way," I chopped at the ice-laden air and indicated the direction.

"Ocht well, alright here, let's try to stay together."

With that we moved cautiously, heads down as we battled on heading west.

Donald was close behind not wanting to get separated when suddenly with no warning the ground beneath him crumbled. He let out a startled yelp and tumbled forward. His arms flailed wildly as he grabbed a handful of my jacket and pulled me sideways. It all happened so fast: In an instant we were hurtling down the icy slope. Desperately, I tried to wield my ice axe, but my arm had caught in something, some part of my jacket. The almost instant surge of adrenalin gave me strength I did not know I had and I broke free and flailed wildly with the axe. Two loud clangs rang in my ears as I hit rock and felt a surge of pain in my wrist; then, with the third strike the axe dug in and provided drag. It twisted me around sharply and as I clung desperately to the handle; it felt like my arm would be pulled from its socket. Tendons strained and the excruciating pain was accompanied by an indecipherable roar of pain.

Then a surge of relief as my momentum slowly eased and I came to a halt, both hands clutched to the axe. I lay there with my face pressed against the icy slope and felt the thunderous beat of my heart like it would burst out of my eardrums or erupt from my chest.

"Scully…" the voice sounded distant and totally impotent against the noise made by the wind, like a freight train passing.

"Donald… you alright? Where the fuck are you?" I yelled and exhaled an enormous sigh of relief as my stomach churned.

"AYE… down here."

"You okay?"

"Ocht it bottoms out; I've not gone over a cliff."

"Thank fuck," I rolled over, tucked the axe firmly under my arm and glissaded down in a cascade of ice and small snowballs. I loomed out of the cloud and slid slowly to a halt next to Donald. He stood taking deep breaths. His legs shook as he brushed ice of his pants and jacket and flexed his shoulder.

"You alright Scully?"

"Aye I managed to stop myself, thought I'd broken my wrist, hit rock with my first two strikes then it dug in. Was almost at the bottom by then!"

"It all happened so quickly, I was just flailing, I grabbed anything I think I pulled you over. For fuck sake, we should not be out here without crampons!"

I put a hand on his shoulder. "C'mon, old soldier, let's get back ti the Bothy." I quickly pulled out the map and reached into my jacket, my heart lurched and my stomach clenched. "*Fuck...* the compass..." I looked around frantically, I could hardly speak.

"Whit where?"

"Must have dropped out when we fell! My arm caught in something..." I replayed the moment in my mind, my heart sinking as the realisation hit. "It must have been the cord!"

"Ohh shite," Donald wailed, then started the futile process of scanning the ground in almost zero visibility. "Ocht it's gone!"

"No here, look!" I took a deep breath, "we must be here somewhere, bottom of a steep slope, if we face the wind we are headed west." I tapped the map and felt more confident. "Aye I think we're here;, wasnae far off, just two three hundred feet lower."

"Aye great but we are *way* off track; should we not be over here?" Donald jabbed at the map.

I scratched my head through the Gore-Tex, and dragged my finger due west across the flapping page. "Well, if we go about three hundred steps and we are here, then the ground should start to rise."

"Aye assuming that *is* where we are, Scully," Donald looked up from the map, peered blindly into the swirling snow and wailed. "Fuck, give us a break!"

"Aye c'mon, let's press on; the ground should rise steeply after a hundred then eh... one, two, three.." Off I went counting out every second step.

I had no backup plan. We were in deep shit, and we both knew it. With a sigh of desperation, Donald fell into line behind me and stomped metronomically in time. We stopped after a hundred steps and squinted into the icy blur.

"It's going up. We could be near the bealach." I pointed at the ground in front of us as my heart rate had calmed slightly.

"Eh...maybe," Donald sounded less convinced.

"C'mon, let's keep goin', at least we are going west, young man!"

Our progress was slow as we grimly counted steps in between arguing intermittently about our exact location. As the ground continued to rise, my confidence grew and the lie of the land seemed to match the contour lines on our map. Then suddenly, for a few brief seconds, the clouds lifted the smooth lines and contours of the hill briefly visible.

"Look!" I shouted, as I pointed about five hundred feet higher to our right: A figure in a bright red Gore-Tex jacket, face covered, stood head down against the wind. He seemed to have a map in hand.

We both yelled and waved. The figure paused as if hearing our faint cries and raised a hand in a clenched fist salute. Then suddenly all was white again.

"Fuck!" I slumped down and pulled out the map. "Donald either they are levitating or that's the Ben and we need to cut much further to the left," I pointed in the direction I thought we should go. "Look, we must be here!"

"Ocht are you sure?"

"Aye, look, it must be Rupert or Liz coming down; either way that's Ben Alder and we are veering way off course. We need to head more this way." I pointed to the left and continued to stare hopefully into the white swirling cloud desperate for another reassuring glimpse of Ben Alder.

"Ocht feck sake, we were going way too far to the right; this wind must be swirling, we must have been heading the wrong way from our first bearing!"

"Aye, fuck a total white out, aided and abetted by some highly magnetised rocks!"

We stood and watched hopefully for another glimpse, confirmation that it was Ben Alder but the wind just lashed us scornfully with icy projectiles.

"Right, let's take it easy and try to walk in a straight line. If the ground doesn't rise soon, then…" My voice trailed off; I left the second part unsaid.

"Ocht aye, stich in nine, as my granny used to say!"

"Did she smell of brandy, piss an' mothballs an' all?"

"Aye, but now don't they all?" We chuckled briefly, gallows humor. "Ocht I just want to get the feck off this hill, Scully, upright and no' in a bag!"

We knew we had reached the bealach when for ten long minutes the funneled wind felt like it could strip flesh from bone. Then, as we dropped down the other side and the ground opened up, it began to ease. Grateful for the respite we hurried on heads down until suddenly we stumbled upon two packs, wedged in behind a rock almost completely buried in the snow.

"It *must* be Rupert and Liz up there; good thing we spotted them that saved us a wee wander." I nodded to the north, "they could be close by!"

"HOOOO!" Donald howled into the wind, and we paused, held our breath and listened intently, but there was no reply. I started to pull the packs out, dusting off the snow.

"What you doing?"

"Acht, making it a wee bit easier for them to find when they get down; they better get a move on, I think this shit is getting worse."

"Aye, indeed good thinking," Donald scanned the white landscape, as I replaced the packs.

"They must have left them here and headed up," I nodded at the packs, "Fuck me, Donald," I pulled out the map, "We were about to veer *way* off course! We almost spent the night at Culra!"

"Aye, assuming we'd have made it that far. I'm knackered: that would have been a cold miserable night."

"Aye, nothing to keep us warm but Jimmy's discarded bottle of pissky. Now c'mon lets just get down out of this stuff!"

"Here," again Donald jabbed at the map. "Assuming we just came through the bealach, we may be coming down the wrong side of the river. It would be safer to double back and cut over."

"Aye, but slower. Are you wanting to spend more time out in this shit?"

"Now then, there is a path there for a reason, Scully!"

"Aye, alright: Compromise, cut straight down, *then* across."

"That is no', a compromise."

"Well you're married, aren't you?" I laughed manically and scratched at my chin, hidden behind a Gore-Tex layer.

"Ocht, fer let's go then, but we should still cross before it gets too steep. I'm not keen on heading down the wrong side of the river, actually wait no!" Donald turned to me his eyes flashed angrily, "I never even wanted to go up the hill. Now feck it, c'mon, let's just cut across now."

With that he tightened his hood ducked down and doggedly headed across the hillside while scanning the snow for danger signs. There was no point in arguing and so with a shrug, I turned and followed.

Suddenly, he was gone.

I froze, my arms flung out briefly, then I moved quickly forward: A huge hole had opened in the snow. I threw myself down, eased towards the gap and peered over. Donald lay on his back on a small ledge holding his sodden wet leg and arm above the river, which flowed past carrying large chunks of ice. Digging my ice axe into the firm ground, I reached down and held out an arm, "here!"

With great care, he slowly eased himself upright his head just poking from the icy cavern. "I'm fine, get out the fuckin' way, Scully!" he screamed angrily, then waved away my hand and crawled out flopping like a Gore-

Tex-clad seal onto the firmer snow on the other side of the hole.

"You alright?"

"Ah, fuckin' told you we should double back then cross over!"

"It would appear that you have!"

"Ocht aye *very fuckin' funny,* I'm soaked; we better get off this hill Scully!" Donald had a tone of fear in his voice.

I bit my lip and said nothing; we were still a long way from the Bothy and there was always the danger of hypothermia. I scrambled over and sat next to him. Suddenly, I remembered something. "Hey, Donald here, look I've got spare mitts."

"Give," he petulantly stretched out a hand.

I dug in my pack and quickly produced a pair of woolen mittens. Snatching them wordlessly, he held one in his left hand, his face racked with pain as he tried to force a claw-like hand, rigid and unyielding, into the mitt. I moved closer and tried to help.

"Fuck off," he angrily whipped his hand away and cursed loudly as he forced his numb hand into the dry glove. As he slowly flexed his hand the look of pain and rage on his face eased as his numb fingers brushed against the warm, dry material. He shoved both hands into his armpits and rocked back and forward hugging himself, his face twisted in pain as the blood flowed once more. I sat to one side and watched silently, face like a scolded dog.

"Ocht well, that's a bit better," Donald's voice sounded more conciliatory as the pain subsided. "Warm hands, feckin' freezing cold wet feet," he managed a weak grin and grabbed his crotch, "acht and my knob's the size of a nipple!"

"Aye, well, no change there, then."

"Ocht away, don't push it, I've not forgiven you yet; I knew we should have gone to the Annoch!"

"Hey, look," I jumped up pointed, a few feet away two sets of footprints looking like they had been made recently led down the hillside. "Could be Robbie and Doc; looks like they got blown off course as well!"

"Ocht aye, maybe," Donald inspected the tracks. "Now, look here, it's like they came from over there so at least *they* had the sense to cross higher up."

I nodded silently, and let him get his little dig in.

"Aye well, let's go; the kettle will be boiled. I can almost taste the Cup-a-Soup!"

A sudden icy blast with some added spindrift acted as a reminder. We quickly covered any exposed skin to avoid additional exfoliation. Then we set off and followed what we assumed were Robbie and Doc's footprints down the hill, back to safety.

17 BURIED PRETTY DEEP

Almost an hour later, we dropped below the clouds. The wind continued to scornfully lash us with sleet as we took the last few exhausted steps to the Bothy and rounded the corner with considerable relief.

We both stopped dead in our tracks.

Sleeping bags and other items lay before us, they smoldered and flapped in the wind like strange dying creatures. It was as if we had stumbled upon a battle scene strewn with the flags of a vanquished army. All that was missing was a lone bugler playing 'Taps'.

"What… the… fuck…?"

We both stared in shock as Robbie and Doc emerged and stumbled from the Bothy coughing, as they dragged the smoking Chesterfield and threw it in the shallow waters. There was a hiss and smoke or steam billowed briefly before being whisked away by the wind. Then they both turned sharply to find us stood stock-still, eyes and mouths wide open..

"Fuckin' WhisperLite blew up…" Doc began, "we saved the Bothy, but most of the gear is fucked."

Donald stooped down, picked up his sleeping bag and examined a huge hole burned through the middle. Burnt and wet duckdown feathers spilled out and fluttered across the ground mingling with the snow, coating the surface of the loch.

"Ah *fuck*…" I sadly shook my head, my shoulders slumping as I noted bits of my gear among the smoking debris.

Doc continued to explain, "must have flooded the priming cap. Fuckin' thing blew up. Next thing we knew, the room was on fire. We managed to smother it before the Bothy went up, but we had to use the bags."

Without a word, Donald dropped his pack and the burnt sleeping bag on the ground. He slowly clenched and unclenched his fists, his face growing red with rage.

Robbie looked like he was about to add something, but stopped and stared in shock as Donald suddenly screamed, "*Ocht why the feck* are you such a fuck up Docherty? Why do you destroy everything you touch?"

"Ho steady now, shut the fuck up… hey!" I was taken aback by the ferocity of Donald's reaction; it seemed a bit premature to be apportioning blame.

"Ocht feck you, Scully, you're just as bad, you almost got me killed up there *twice!*"

"Hey fuck off yah wee fat cunt, *it was a fuckin' accident!*" Doc advanced, his eyes flashed angrily as he shoved a sooty chin bristling with three days of stubble right into Donald's face.

"*Feck you!*" Donald screamed, and shoved Doc, who staggered back, slipping on the wet icy ground and falling heavily against the Bothy. He looked shocked, like an old man being knocked over, flailing desperately, almost sadly, the muscle memory of his athletic youth a faded recollection. He quickly recovered though, scrambling to his feet and lurching forward, throwing a wild punch that missed its intended target. He kept coming as Donald dropped a shoulder and shoved him back. More punches flailed through the snow making infrequent contact before Doc again slipped on the icy ground and fell heavily.

Sensing his chance Donald sprang forward aiming a kick, his huge heavy hiking boot swinging in an arc towards Doc's head. A fraction of a second before the bone-cracking impact, I sprang forward and shoved Donald. His balance was off, he careened down the slope towards the loch and rolled into the reedy grass.

"Hey… c'mon ti *fuck* you two!" I screamed, my heart pounding wildly; the sudden rush of adrenaline had swept away any feeling of cold. I moved quickly to position myself between them and raised my hands trying to act as the peacemaker.

Donald scrambled to his feet ready to charge back up the bank then froze; there was a knife in Doc's hand.

"Right, yah wee fat bastard, c'mon, let's fuckin' do this!"

"Hoh fuckin' behave Doc; you an' all Doughboy," I took another step and danced around as I tried to keep between the pair, my heart almost beating out my chest.

"Get oot the fuckin' way, Scully, or I'll jib you n' all!"

"Aye shift, Scully; now c'mon, baldy cunt!"

Donald scrambled over to his pack and grabbed his ice axe. Doc circled menacingly, his teeth bared like a wild animal, crouched ready to spring. I twisted and turned my arms out acting as a barrier between the pair as they sought an opening. Doc made a half-hearted lunge then jumped back and watched Donald closely with beady dark eyes.

The wind was still ferociously whipping both snow and smoke so the icy snowball seemed to come out of nowhere. It hit Doc just below the chin and exploded upwards with an invigorating chill. He recoiled, took several steps back and searched for the source, as a second snowball hit Donald square on the side of his head then a third hit Doc on the shoulder, and sent a shower of ice into his ear.

"Fer fuck, *fuck off,* Robbie," Doc screamed.

Robbie strode into view, clutching two large icy snowballs, "well put the weapons *down* then, yah daft bastards!"

Donald cowered and held up the ice axe as if it was a crucifix, and he had to defend himself from the devil, as Robbie gestured as if to nail him point blank.

"*Aye,* put them down," I stooped and quickly grabbed large chunks of icy snow arming myself ready to hit the first one who moved. "Both of you!"

"*Fuck you!*" Doc screamed, throwing down the knife; it stuck shuddering in the frozen ground and he strode angrily off, quickly disappeared into the swirling snow.

"Hey Doc, c'mon, wait…"

"Leave him, Robbie, leave him… he needs to calm down." I turned to Donald, "you too, turn it down, eh…?"

"Feck you," Donald snarled as he threw down the ice axe and headed into the Bothy.

"Fuck I'm no' playing rock paper scissors with you, snowballs eh…" I looked around at the burnt gear still breathing heavily as I felt my heartbeat recede. "Fuck, they were like a pair of yappy wee dogs! Now, what happened, Robbie?"

"Dunno!" he wailed, "we had a Cup-a-Soup, put more water on the boil for you two, then came outside; we were stood out here looking up the hill, trying to decide if we had to come and look for you, when *boom,* fuckin' thing went up. We both charged back in and did what we could to stop the place burning to the ground; we had to use the bags to put out the flames. The fuel had sprayed everywhere, desperate stuff, so it was. It was all still smoldering, so we threw stuff in the river or chucked water over it. Jeez, but ma heart's still fit to burst out my chest Scully." Robbie paused and took a deep breath, "Eh… what happened with Donald?"

"Aye… we got a bit lost in the whiteout, he took a header, pulled me down; we had to ice axe arrest, lost the compass, nae batteries in the GPS. Then when we finally found our way to the path, we started coming down the wrong side, eh… my idea. When we tried to cross over, he went through a snow bridge into the river."

"Ah well, that explains why he wasnae in a very good mood. We did something similar: Came down through these deep gulley chest deep in the snow. I had to sort of swim across the top but kept sinking in. I was soaked, so was Doc; we were done in by the time we got back, but the wee adrenaline rush fi being firemen soon got us back on our feet again."

"Tooled up, though, heh…? I stooped down to pick up Doc's knife. "Pair of fuckin' bams!"

Then I threw the snowball in the river grabbed the Bothy book and followed Robbie inside.

Donald seemed to have calmed down some as he swept water and burnt plastic out of the room into the hallway as thick acrid smoke billowed out the door.

"You alright Donald?" Robbie still sounded breathless.

"Ocht aye I'm fine, just mad as hell; bad day at the orifice, I'll calm down in a bit." He avoided eye contact and continued sweeping.

"C'mon Donald, it was an accident; dinnae go blaming Doc. I mean, you're right to be hacked off at me, I… I should've listened to you."

"Ocht feck it, just feck it," Donald threw down the broom, sat on the bench and surveyed the room. Grimly he noted the burn marks up the wall and the gobs of molten plastic that had solidified on the floor. "Pulling a knife on me though, what the feck, eh?"

"Aye, you can take the man out of Glasgow, cannae take Glasgow out the man. Anyway, think there may have been a bit of excess adrenaline; I wouldnae take it personally." I stared silently at the scorched walls of the Bothy and digested the stark realisation; the consequence of what had just happened.

Donald slowly raised his head, "ocht what happened, Robbie?"

"Acht… we'd put more water on and come out to look for you two, heard a bang when we got back in, and the place was blazing. Fuel sprayed everywhere, we just wanted to make sure you boys had a cup of tea."

"Aye… ocht well," suddenly Donald looked less pissed off, perhaps the realisation that they had actually been concerned about us, and not just stupid or careless. "Ocht well, at least we have our packs and boots; it could be a lot worse."

"Aye, it's actually no' too bad," Robbie tried to force a positive note in his voice. "All the sleeping bags are gone, and stuff on the drying rack is either minging or a bit burnt, but all in all, boots gaiters, wet gloves, and hey, at least the floor will be clean!"

"Aye, true, nae one died," I inspected the Bothy book.

"Ocht fer, is it toast as well?"

"No' too bad," I teased open the pages. "This page is the worst." I held the book open, the ink had run merging the letters and words into one large indecipherable smear. "It's a bit singed and charred but acht it'll be alright." I stood it on top of the stove carefully separated out the pages then grabbed the Jetboil stove and moved through to the other room to make more tea. I even managed a weak smile as Robbie ruefully shouted, "Oh hey Scully, be careful!"

At least the other room did not smell too badly of burnt plastic, and once the tea was ready we discussed our options.

"I'm seriously knackered; not looking forward to that climb across the moor into the forest, the snows going to be deep, but its no' going to get any easier…" I nodded out the window at the snow, "But could be even worse tomorrow."

"Aye, well, maybe it's time to pack up and get out of Dodge, It's going to be a slog." Robbie paused as Doc reappeared and shuffled silently into the room.

"Tea?" I held out the cup. "Eh, we're just discussing *our* options."

"Ta," Doc took the cup and studied the contents.

A moment of tense silence followed until Donald coughed lightly, "Hey Doc eh…." he stopped and shrugged.

"Aye, fuck it, Donald, ah was being pretty daft n' all…"

"Tooled up, eh…? What a pair, right, shake on it and move on?" Robbie looked at each in turn, slowly and simultaneously their hands met accompanied by a pair of muttered grunts.

Robbie looked pleased, "*right* now the topic is should we stay or should we go."

"Well my t'pence worth is we have no choice. I'm no' staying without a bag unless we go get a lot more wood, keep the fire blazing all night!" I looked at Doc then Donald, both sat in silent contemplation.

"Aye, I agree, Scully, there could be another foot of snow by tomorrow!"

"Ocht but we'll have fresh legs, it's going to be a real struggle if we go now!"

The impasse brought a silence as we each thoughtfully studied our cups or looked out the window.

Finally I spoke, "Well, my vote is still we go for it, thanks to our wee mishap the packs are light and the snow could get deeper. I'm no' sure a night huddled by the fire will make us feel any fresher!"

Robbie nodded slowly, "well I'm with Scully, but I don't feel too bad; my legs are still fresh."

"Ocht yah young bastard, my wee short legs will no keep up with your strides!"

"Eh, here hold on, you're no' thinking of trying ti make ti the train, are you?"

"Aye, good point, Doc, we'll be toiling to make that," Robbie's shoulders slumped, "we dinnae want a repeat of the Fifties."

"Well, one option we can *all* squeeze inti the van; if we leave soon we'll get a few miles in before darkness. But it's going ti be tough going through the forest."

"Aye, yeah reckon so," Robbie slowly added, "Eh... mind you, if we do that it'll cost us two pairs of shoes and *four* cans of beer."

I nodded towards the room at the other end of the short corridor. "Aye, there's also a litre bottle of Asda whisky and a few cans of beer left over, but we can drink the cans."

"Well I'm no' lugging the whisky back out again!" Doc declared.

"Aye, well we could bury the whisky in a safe place, it'll be fine, eh...?"

"Until next year," Robbie finished off my statement.

"Aye," I agreed, "least of our worries, well we better no' hang about as Doc said it will be dark by the time we reach the forest; we can bury stuff or bag it and leave it for the MBA boys, but we'd better get a shift on!"

"Ocht aye," Donald sighed and nodded, then looked at Doc.

"Aye well, I don't think we've much choice, Donald, fuck it, let's go!"

I jumped to my feet and slammed my empty teacup on the windowsill to emphasise that the choice had been made. There was a short pause, then a flurry of activity as we each considered items and discarded gear that was burnt or would not be to sorely missed.

Doc picked up the charred remnants of the WhisperLight and hung it on a nail by the side of the window as if to act as a warning to others.

Robbie lit a fire; the flames rapidly consumed the remaining food, no doubt disappointing the Bothy mice. Then we circled around, our heavy boots thumped noisily as we examined any items revealed as gear was packed. Gradually, each filled pack moved outside and rested above the snow on the bench, now sadly back to being a Chippendale. On no time at all the room had returned to the barren spartan state we had found it in.

I grabbed a worn out brush and swept the floor as Donald shoveled the debris into the fire; we did not speak, we just went through the motions. There was something slightly unreal about the situation. The premature end to this year's trip hung in the air, undeniable and inevitable.

Donald shut the glass doors and pushed down firmly on the latch. Straightening up, he looked around the room, then gently picked up the Bothy book. "Ocht here now I'm not putting our names to this debacle," he mumbled softly and ripped out the damaged page on which Robbie had recorded the weekend's events, the ink now smeared like tear-stained mascara.

"Well then, that's us; I think we're almost all set!" I made one last scan of the room. Smoke billowed behind the glass door and streamed gently up the chimney, the embers safely contained inside the stove.

"Aye all set?" I asked as Robbie returned with the shovel.

"Aye, dug a hole, buried most of it; just one bag for the MBA boys!"

"Right then," we stepped outside; the wind had dropped slightly and the snow was still falling heavily.

"Oh here better take careful note of that spot, lads!" Robbie pointed through the thick white flakes. A few hundred yards away Doc shoveled frozen dirt. In palpable silence, we watched as he gently trod the dirt, replaced the frozen sod and picked up a small rock to mark the spot. He began to take very precise strides to the base of a more prominent rock, then seemingly satisfied, turned and headed back to the Bothy.

"Alright?"

"Eh... aye, fuck, it's well hid, buried pretty deep once you get through the frigging permafrost, the soil's easy ti shift." He pointed in the direction of the rock. "Exactly seven paces due south of that one, under a small boulder, one litre bottle Asda malt, wrapped in a slightly singed sleeping bag ti keep it warm."

"Eh right then eh... photo?"

"C'mon then, make it snappy young Robs, and here, get eh.... that rock in the background. We can refresh our ageing memories, for eh..." I hesitated briefly then quietly added, "next year."

"Aye well, that and the chance of another temperature inversion are all the incentive I need, but it's a good idea to get it in a photo. Last thing I want is to waste time digging under every boulder that's seven steps south of a large rock!"

Doc placed the shovel in the porch, pulled the main door firmly shut and joined the line as Robbie set up his camera. The last can of beer was passed around and Robbie waved his hand to indicate how we should line up before he strode quickly over to take his place.

"Oh hey say cheese you old farts."

Then everyone except Robbie sucked in their stomach as a small light flashed and the sliding click announced that four smiles each as tinged as the Bothy book had been captured for posterity.

"Well then we eh... best get fuckin' going eh!" Doc strode towards the river and splashed across. He paused on the far bank then marched on without a backwards glance.

"Right then!"

"Ocht aye, sure fer sure," Donald quickly drained the can of beer dropped it on the ground, crushed it flat with the heel of his boot and flicked it to me. I deftly slipped it unnoticed into the outside pocket of Robbie's pack.

Crossing the second river, we fanned out across the hill each trying to find the easiest path. I strained up the last few steps to the stand of pines and stopped.

Doc stood and stared into the clouds and mumbled, "fuck… shite."

"Acht, accidents happen, we had our fun yesterday. Nae worries, at least we didnae burn it down, it'll be there next year and we get to come back!"

"Aye," Doc nodded, "job done, eh?"

"Yeah, that was great, glad that worked out so well, unforgettable day, things kind of got weird after that though did they, no'?"

Doc sighed, "acht, c'mon ti fuck, yer sounding like Doughboy!"

I did not respond, I was staring at the Bothy, sat in its isolated location. It looked so solid and safe, impervious to the wind and snow.

"Anyway, fuck it, you know what is weird what makes no sense? That stove, It's never done anything like that!"

"Thought you said it was the priming cap?"

"Aye but it was already lit; we'd had a cuppa. It should've been primed!"

"Acht, it was getting old, like us."

"Makes no sense…" His voice trailed off, "here, eh… did you sign the Bothy book?"

"Nah," I nodded at the approaching figure of Donald, "he ripped out this year's entry, didnae want the MBA boys knowing it was us."

Robbie and Donald climbed the last few steps to the stand of pines and we stood huddled in the swirling snow.

"Fuck," Doc turned to look down the loch, "I'm no' looking forward ti this."

"Acht it'll be fine," I tried to muster a cheerful note in my voice as I banished the memories of the struggle we'd had getting in.

"Aye well, at least the bog will be frozen and the paths okay; well, until the forest, so eh… until next year then?"

Although the swirling snow partly obscured the view far to the west, a dark patch indicated the solid tree cover that stretched across the horizon.

"Ocht well, now you know how the Hobbits felt when they saw Milkwood." Donald shouted as he strode off followed by Robbie.

Doc stopped lit a cigarette and held out the pack to me, "you want?" He paused and frowned, "eh here was it no' Mirkwood?"

"Aye, ta!"

We stood and watched as they crossed the bog, moving easily over the frozen ground. "Well, he's the right shape fur a Hobbit," I noted then turned to look back across the glen at the Bothy. "Here, ever wonder what the guys who built it looked like, Doc?"

"Hard a fuck!" he growled.

"Aye," I chuckled; he'd hit the nail on the head, Victorian laborers no doubt clad in tweed, toiling in all weathers, working the granite and slate with their sweat and bloodied knuckles. Their labor was long before the digital age, their thousand-yard stares unrecorded. Their legacy though still stood in rugged granite testament.

Maybe next year, we would all return, or perhaps some simple twist of fate like Banjo's bike crash would end the journey for one or all. The Bothy though, well, that would still be here, it was going nowhere. In this inhospitable climate it couldn't even gather moss, perhaps it would just collect a few more ghosts.

I shivered, turned my back on the only sanctuary for miles around and trudged after Doc.

18 ROLL YOUR SLEEVES UP

The heavily falling snow accentuated the silence as we marched along the side of the loch, in single file, focused on getting back to the van, no stops for photos or taking in the scenery. We did stop at the river for a brief respite and leant our packs on the low handrail of the bridge as chocolate was passed around, and the somber line masticated in unison.

Ben Alder was gone, shrouded in a monochrome sky that now blended seamlessly into the waters of Loch Ericht as the darkness rolled ominously in.

Doc dropped his pack and headed for the cover of some trees, toilet paper in one hand cigarette in the other and we pushed on. We walked side by side on a Land Rover track squinting into the snow flurries that obscured our view.

Robbie sighed.

"Ocht disappointing eh?"

"Aye well, a wee bit, bit of a sad end especially after yesterday, I was looking forward to another night."

"Aye there's always next year, Robbie!"

"Ocht aye well, it will be good to get home, see Sarah and the laddie."

Robbie frowned thoughtfully and looked doubtful. "Aye well it'll probably still be pretty frosty, things are no' so good."

"Oh aye, is wee Colin still being a handful then eh?" Donald grinned.

"No eh, I've met someone else, someone I can have more of a laugh with, since then things have really gone downhill."

There was silence as Donald's brow furrowed darkly and he considered the information. He glanced at me, "you'd had this news flash then?" He didn't wait for my reply. "Well, is this serious, is it?"

"Well its, eh... she's just more fun."

"Ocht aye, well, hard to be fun when you've been spending time potty training or you're knackered through sleep depravation and constantly doing the laundry!" There was a deeply sarcastic tone to Donald's voice.

"Its no' just that I mean she's," Robbie's voice haltered and he looked at me. I had already decided to keep quiet.

"No up to her elbows in domestic shite, perhaps," Donald spat back crisply, Robbie bit his lip. "Now listen Robbie, Sarah is a fine lass; things will get easier, just give it time. It was really hard going with me an Mhari for the longest time, just don't go doing anything rash. The grass always seems greener you know."

"Eh aye, Doc said something like that!"

"Oh fer *feck sake!*" Robbie recoiled, startled by the venom of the expletive outburst.

Donald took a deep breath, looked over his shoulder, and continued in a more measured voice. "Fer fecksake Robbie, look, Doc is still one of my best mates, even if I'm pretty pissed off at him. Regardless, let me give you a wee word of advice. Do not be looking to him for pointers when it comes to marriage and Scully here is not much better!"

"Ho steady yah wee shite, for your information I told him he should work at it and leave the wee floozy to the next customer."

"Aye… well, fair enough fair enough, sorry but sometimes I feel I'm the only one who ever gives *sensible* advice."

"Aye, like, have another?" I snorted.

Donald ignored me and raged on, "Ocht the problem is, Doc should never have married that miserable whining lassie. One day he will wise up and get the feck out, cause he's depressed enough as it is, and he's not getting any happier! You know the real tragedy of what just happened back there in the Bothy is he is the one person who needed this break the most; it was going to be one of the few bright spots of his year!"

Drops of spittle flew from Donald's lips into the snowy sky. The tirade looked set to continue so we walked silently on, Robbie darting glances, waiting to see if the outburst was over.

"Ocht anyway, Robbie, I'm getting off topic. Thing is, try to do yourself a favour and stick to happily married people if you want to know the best way to try an fix yours!" With that, Donald fell silent and trudged in lock step next to Robbie.

"I never realized you didnae like Susie!"

"Ocht she's no so bad, I'll live to be a hundred and I'll still never understand why nice girls marry bad boys and think they're going to change them! Fer sure she should never have married Doc or he shouldnae have married her. It's not like they make each other happy, and now with the twins they've made that choice even harder." Donald waved a gloved hand swatting snowflakes in exasperation. "Now, I never felt that way about you and Sarah, you pair used to have a ball. That ability just gets buried in the shite that life and kids throws at you!"

"Eh… does that mean you never thought Sarah was a nice girl?"

Donald's irate expression mellowed, "Ocht, well she didn't seem to mind getting a bit dirty as I recall."

Robbie flicked a gloved hand in my direction. "Fuck, that's what he said an' all, you boys have got a funny fuckin' opinion of my wife."

"Ocht aye look here, Robbie, there's still gold in there, just roll your sleeves up and get digging!"

"Aye well, you know what, *you* should team up wi her, Donald, she's the one who fancies her chances as a fuckin' guidance counsellor!"

"Ocht, whit?"

"Aye, she's got time to go and sit and listen to her cousin Pete while he warbles about his fuckin' lack of marital bliss. I told her, perhaps its cause he's an idiot, that's why his wife kicked him out and he has to sleep on some mate's sofa in some shithole. But oh no, she'll go off and traipse into town and sit there listening to him crying into his beer!"

"Ocht aye fer feck are you not feeling wanted?" Donald gave Robbie a withering glance. "Well maybe if you paid *her* a wee bit more attention instead of hanging around with your wee bit on the side!"

The comment hung accusingly in the snowy sky.

"When was last time you took her out?"

"Aye well, there's a couple of decent bands coming up, but as I said to him, she'll no leave the wee fella alone with any of the locals."

"Ah c'mon ti fuck Robbie, they cannae all be glue-crazed neds?"

"You've no' been to my house have you, Scully?"

"Ocht here, Robbie, you should use your powers of persuasion, think of wee Colin! Why take a gamble that the alternative would make you happy, when you know it might not turn out that way?"

"Aye Donald, but what if it does and I didnae take the chance?" Robbie's sharp response and his perceived dilemma seemed to stun Donald into silence, then he retorted, switching the focus. "Here have you ever told Doc what you think, and here, what about you, Scully, what do you think of her?"

"Em…" I glanced quickly over my shoulder Doc was still some distance behind us doggedly trudging up the path, the dark sky behind seemed an appropriate backdrop. "Well, Donald is right, she's a miserable cow, but as I recall she was always like that, so I'm no' sure if life with the dark prince has made her any better or worse." Robbie laughed nervously at this the one nickname we rarely used, as Doc tended to go ballistic when he heard himself called that.

"Ocht anyway," Donald chimed in again, "why tell him what he already knows? Why do you think he is always so keen to do stuff like this? See, now the past is just a way better country for our boy Doc; don't be going down that road, Robbie!"

I suppressed a snort at the ironic comment while Robbie sighed deeply and looked pensive, eyes fixed on the ground.

A few moments later we reached the point where the path turned sharply and cut straight up towards the highest point on the moor. We caught our breath and steeled ourselves for the long slog up the hill.

"You got any water?" I sucked fruitlessly on my CamelBak, the tube even with the winter cover on it, was frozen solid.

"Shite, no, mine's the same," Robbie readily eased off his pack and grabbed a bottle from the side pocket, clearly eager to end or change the conversation. "I'll fill up down there. Any other bottles?"

And with that Robbie headed down to the river.

"Alright?" Doc growled as he approached, I watched him closely for signs that he may have heard my comment or Donald's sage advice, but he seemed his usual grumpy self: No better, no worse.

"Ocht, here, we better take some of this," Donald passed around his hip flask, "keep us warm while we wait."

Suddenly, there was a loud crack: the unmistakable sound of ice breaking, followed by a yell as Robbie went through into the ice-cold water.

"*Fuck!*" the cry rang out in unison as we dropped our packs sprang down the hill and reached Robbie moments later. He had crawled onto the riverbank having gone thigh deep into the water. Pulling him quickly from the river we climbed back up to the path.

"*Shite!*" Robbie screamed as he removed his boots and poured at least a pint of icy water out of each. "Anyone got dry socks?"

"Aye... slightly smoky and sweaty, but dry," Doc began to rummage in his pack, "I've nae spare leggings though!"

Robbie quickly switched socks, shoved his feet into the boots and grimaced as he felt the squelch of ice cold wet leather, "Oh fuck..."

There was silence as we watched, I could not think of a single positive thing to say, the usual recourse to gallows humour was not an option. Here, at the halfway point with miles to go there was no point in turning back and no means of lighting a fire on the exposed moor.

I turned and looked up the hill the beam of light from my torch picked out the relative smoothness of the path, contrasting sharply with the dappled tapestry of rocks and tufts of grass on either side. An undulating smooth white line seemed to stretch forever, upwards into the dark snowy sky.

Without a word Robbie turned and began the long slow slog to the highpoint of the moor.

We followed in silence, four lonely circles of light that danced and bobbed across the dark hillside.

Cresting the highest point, we dropped down and approached the forest. Robbie stopped and sheltered from the steady wind that moved the drifting deepening snow. To my alarm, as we passed around a water bottle I noticed that he was already shivering, so I forged quickly ahead into the darkness.

Gradually, we formed a line and the others stepped knee deep into my footsteps. 'Post holing' is the Sunday name for this technique; total fucking torture is what it should be called. Groaning, sweating and exhausted, I ground to a halt, hands on my knees.

Doc and Donald both tried to go to the front at the same time. "I'll take this one, Donald," Doc mumbled softly.

"Ocht right behind you," Donald responded as he fell into line, and the high stepping stomp through the knee-deep snow continued. Four hundred steps move to the left next man up and repeat, and so the exhausting relay continued without respite. As another steep rise approached, we dug once more into the reserves of aching muscle. Each of us in our own private world of pain, aware of the consequences; there was no way we could stop: We had to push on.

At the head of the group Doc paused and considered the latest hill as the wind shook the trees and mockingly dropped more snow in our path. Exhausted, we waited for what seemed like an eternity, breathing heavily, unable to take another step, it seemed that spent fuel was all we had. Donald raised his head and looked at me then Robbie; we just stood hands on knees, the silence broken only by deep gasps and groans. I realised I was feeling warm, and fought off a rising urge just to lie down in the snow, curl up and go to sleep.

"Here izat," Robbie slurred as he looked into the forest, "Izat a light? I think there may be a house over there!"

"Ocht here Robbie," Donald shot a concerned glance in my direction. "Robbie we're in the middle of the forest, there's no house there!"

"Aye here, Robbie, c'mon it's this way!"

"Naw, naw, I can see a light," Robbie pulled off his hat and stood upright as if to get a better look. "It must be a wee house; there's probably a toasty wee fire an…" He took a few haltering steps off the path into the deeper snow.

"Ocht *Robbie,*" Donald grabbed him by the shoulder and shouted, "There's no house, nothing, we're in the forest, we *have* to go this way!"

I jumped over to join Donald, Robbie had taken off one of his gloves and claimed he felt warm. He was not getting warm. What he was, was showing early signs of hypothermia. I grabbed his hand, "Robbie, mate, put the glove back on, *please!*"

"Ocht Robbie come on!" Donald tried to shove him towards the path.

"Ah ti fuck, *fuck you*, c'mon then, *let's fuckin' do this!*"

We turned in shock as Doc screamed out the oath at the hill, at the forest, at the deep snow and at the prospect of defeat. It was something he'd screamed many times before, in bar fights, on the football field, whenever, wherever, he'd faced and defeated his toughest adversaries. As we watched, mouths agape, he started to pound and kick the snow cursing repeatedly.

I straightened up took a deep breath summoned what reserves I had left and shoved Robbie hard. At first, he seemed confused but then he jumped after Doc and we followed close behind.

Now we had a rhythm and an unrelenting pace, on we marched, it was brutal, aching muscles competed with the cries of pain, oaths and screams of rage. Every swearword, every fuckin' curse we had ever heard and a few that morphed right there on the spot were spat venomously at the snowy path as on we stomped.

Time seemed to blur with the swirling snow caught in the four bobbing weaving beams of light. Each icy breath felt like it would shatter my aching lungs like breaking glass.

Then suddenly, we reached the end.

The forest opened out and the path crossed onto flat open moor. With huge relief, we found that the deep snow had been blown so it drifted until it was only a few inches deep on the windward side.

"Fuck, but we are out of the woods!" shouted Doc triumphantly.

"Ocht downhill for the rest of it!" Donald agreed as he slapped Doc happily on the shoulder.

I just walked slowly in circles, hands on hips, taking deep agony filled gasps in relief and howling softly at the pain, I just wanted to cry. Robbie leant against the fence and drooled, exhausted.

Finally, as the gasps and groans died down, Doc turned back to the forest, the light from his torch flickered across the deep snow and the tracks we had left behind. "Fuck you… just, fuck you!" he muttered softly and raised a middle finger defiantly. Then he turned and grabbed Robbie, who followed obediently half staggering, half marching by his side as they headed down the hill across the moor.

"Phew, now that was a close one, eh? The wee pugnacious bastard has his uses." Donald exhaled in an exhausted snort. Then as he noticed I had a smile on my face through eyes were filled with sweat and tears, he demanded, "Ocht here, now whit, the feck' are *you* grinning about?"

"Eh...? What nothin', nothin'," I stammered, a little embarrassed, caught in a private moment.

"Nothing, *Aye*... really?"

"Eh... ah fuck it!" I watched as Robbie and Doc pounded down the hill, then with a sheepish grin I explained. "Eh.... I just got a picture of Angie sat in a sunny room curled up with a hot cocoa, wearing just her nightie. It was, eh... taking my mind off the pain."

"Ocht evi-feckin'-dently," Donald laughed, "ha, bet you don't tell her half the stories you tell us lot."

"Ah...abso-fuckin'-lutely not, ah do all my best reminising at the Bothy!"

"Ocht aye, it's good to have," he nodded happily. "Now c'mon Scully, let's get out of here, before Mother Nature thinks of something else to slap our sorry arses with!"

"Aye, with you there old soldier, with you there!"

The weather seemed to accept defeat, and the thick heavy snowflakes that swirled down only coated our packs lightly as we strode across the moor.

"Ocht now, that's got to be the most eventful one ever; I think we just got a wee slap there for taking things for granted!"

"Aye," I looked somberly at Donald as I considered the day we had just had, and some of the stranger goings-on, especially up on the hill. Then I thought of Rupert and Liz and shuddered. "Here, hope they made it to Culra!"

Through the weak light of our head torches, the van came into view. The figure of Doc stood and watched the path, a cigarette hanging from his lips, shoulders hunched, hands deep in his pockets. Robbie was in the front seat extracting warmth from the dashboard vent as steam billowed from the vans exhaust.

"Ocht now, yah beauty!' Donald smiled, "that *is* a welcome sight!"

Robbie sported a mismatched selection of dry clothes. Doc's spare pants were just a little on the short side but he had stopped shivering and perked up noticeably.

Doc eased the van back and accelerated as the tone of the engine indicated the wheels had hit a patch of ice. Switching rapidly from reverse to first then back again he rolled the van backwards and forward. However, even with the extra weight it could not gain enough purchase. After much squealing and rocking it became clear we would make no further progress.

"Right, better get out and put some weight on the front," Doc shouted.

"Oh, fer fucks sake," I grumbled, as we extricated ourselves and pushed down hard or kicked stones and dirt under the front tires.

Suddenly, the van lurched back, freed from the icy trap; simultaneously, Doc spun the wheel and stomped on the brakes, the Vauxhall pirouetted smoothly and came to a halt facing the road.

We squeezed back in and had barely shut the doors before the van sprang forward eagerly, headed for the Stable Bar and the promise of refreshment.

19 NINE O'CLOCK NEWS

As we reached Kinlochrannoch, Robbie's phone finally located a signal and began to vibrate and buzz furiously.

'Fuck me, Sarah has called like, twenty times. Must be trouble in Dodge." He quickly jabbed buttons on his phone and held put it to his ear. "Hey there, its me."

Sarah's voice could clearly be heard on the other end, she was screaming hysterically

"Oh hey there hey c'mon we're fine"

Sarah took a deeper breath and calmed down slightly but then told Robbie not to tell her to bloody calm down and that two climbers had been killed on Ben Alder on Saturday and how she was sick with worry and how she couldn't get hold of him and thought he had been dead. She sobbed ;loudly as Robbie just held a hand across his moth and stared in shock

"Hey, hey, hey, we're fine, really fine. Saturday, you say? Are you sure?"

Robbie continued his conversation as Doc pulled into the car park behind the Stable Bar, the illuminated Tennants Beer sign shone like a welcoming beacon that summoned the thirsty.

"Oh hey hey Doc a wait a minute, are you sure we should be stopping, should we no get home?"

"Ah fuck off getting home an hour sooner will no make any difference." And with that we jumped out the car.

"Hasnae yet made the news in Boston," I commented as I checked my phone. "What a shame, eh? Saturday was such a perfect day as well."

"Aye," Doc grumbled, "I'll give Susie another few minutes of hope before I deliver the bad news that I'm still alive!"

"Tsk… oh fer fucksake Doc, c'mon, let's get a beer."

"Aye, fuck each!"

And off he went, doddering like an old man across the gravel car park on tight muscles and blistered feet.

It was warm and cozy inside, a coal fire blazed in the hearth, and a row of customers sat hunched at the bar watching TV in bored silence.

The barman, a stocky fellow with the ruddy complexion of a man whose face was no stranger to the Highland wind summed us up in an instant. He moved swiftly, one hand on a beer tap as the other hovered near the pint glasses.

"What you having?" Doc asked as he examined the beer taps.

"Ehh… Belhaven Best for me!"

"Aye," Doc nodded at the barman, "two Belhaven, make one a shandy."

"Do you do tea or coffee?" Robbie looked hopefully at the barman.

"Naw," the one word answer was abrupt and final.

"Ocht aye, well, better make that two Guinness then!"

As he swiftly filled a pint glass halfway with lemonade, his hands moved fluently like a conductor of some bizarre orchestra, flicking one tap to halt the flow of Guinness while he flipped another to fill a second glass with beer.

With an idle fascination, I watched the curiously hypnotic dance of bubbles that swirled up and down the glass as the Guinness settled and changed in hue from brown, to black and white. Satisfied that the barman clearly knew his trade, the others hobbled over and sat at a table, partially encircled by a padded leather bench. They slid into the seats with a chorus of appreciative groans, stretched out their legs and luxuriated in the relative comfort.

"Is that all?"

"Aye eh," Doc licked his lips, "an' gi'es four bags of crisps, any flavour."

Doc and I sat and stared blankly at the television as Robbie mumbled softly to himself and scanned his e-mails.

As he finished his conversation, Donald placed his phone gently down on the table and coughed lightly. "Ocht Mhari says the police just told her that the climbers did fall on Saturday but they where from England: St Andrews University. So she knew it wasn't us, but she's not that happy, to say the least. Might be tricky getting a pass for next year!"

"Acht, that's a long time off, she'll have forgotten. What a bummer though, such a cracking day an all." I shook my head sadly, we did not known them, we had never met them, but we knew why they had been there. A mutual love of the hills in winter.

"Aye, conditions were perfect an all. Here, you don't think they were blinded by a big cloud of Banjo ash blowing off the top, do you?" Doc managed to look both appalled and delighted at this suggestion as Donald shook his head in irritation.

Suddenly Robbie laughed, "oh hey good news, she forgot to mention that, but cousin Pete is back with his wife!" He took a large gulp of his beer and announced, "Well, time to drop the kids off at the pool!"

"Eh? Cousin Pete?" Doc queried, but Robbie had already departed through the door at the back of the bar marked 'Toilet.'

"Ocht, eh… it seems Sarah has had a pet project counselling her loser of a cousin while he sniveled into his beer about his marital problems; poor Robbie wasn't feeling loved. Seems she was spending too much time listening to his woes and not concentrating on Robbie."

"Here?" I glanced sideways at Doc something had occurred to me, "em this counselling wasnae in the Tass by any chance, was it?"

"Ocht, I dunno, you heard him too…" Donald gave me one of his withering quizzical glances to indicate he felt I was getting off topic. "Ocht why do you ask?"

"Acht nutin' maybe just a case of mistaken identity."

Re-emerging a few minutes later, Robbie slid quickly into his seat with a guilty look on his face. "Phew, wouldnae go in the bogs for a while, aye cracked the windy open but eh… that one would gag a maggot!"

"Fer fuck sake," Doc shook his head, "here Robbie, where was yer cousin Pete staying?"

"Eh… a sofa in his mate's place, some dive on Jeffreys Street."

"Eh…" Doc's voice sounded even gruffer than usual, "I think I might have seen him and Sarah one night, in the Tass."

"Aye quite possibly. Hopefully we've seen the last of that though, she's giving the counselling game a miss! Quiet night in tonight, long shower, get myself clean, then who knows eh?" Robbie rubbed his hands and looked pleased.

"Well an extra night in Embra' suits me an all, more of my ma's cooking."

"Well fuck that, Susie will be asleep by nine; if we're heading back ti Embra' I'm no' back ti work yet, so I'm heading out tomorrow, check out who's playing Bannermans. Do you no' fancy that, Robbie, maybe with a wee pint before?" Doc flashed Robbie a wicked and knowing grin that morphed into a disappointed sneer as Robbie just shook his head. He turned to me, "how 'bout you Scully?"

"Well I'm knackered at the moment. Sleep and my ma's cooking is all I can think of, but I suppose I'll be rested enough by tomorrow!"

"Aye good man!"

Donald stood up, groaned loudly, "Ocht now then… one for the road, or are we in a big hurry?"

"Aye, what the fuck no' that much of a rush."

"Same again?" he groaned bitterly, "ocht now, it is *shite* getting old!"

"Aye ta, old me? Hah I'm feeling brand new!" Robbie happily lied.

"Aye, did you check yer pack, yah young pup? It might be full of snowballs?"

"Eh… what? You better no' have…" Robbie looked sharply at me then Doc, we both just laughed as Donald hobbled stiffly to the bar and nodded curtly at the barman.

We took a bit more time with the second pint, savouring the beer more, our thirst quenched by the rapid consumption of the first. The mood continued to be somber as much as from exhaustion as from having left the Bothy a day early, gradually though, our spirits lifted.

"Here, eh… Doc, meant to ask you before, but how'd you get that scar?" Robbie pointed at a faded crescent-shaped scar on Doc's hand.

"Aye," Doc sighed, "That was me trying ti preserve Banjo's eh… good looks."

"Aye? How'd that work out then?"

"Eh… I was out drinking wi' him in a dive of a pub down Leith Walk. I'd just gone ti the bar ti get them in, trying to catch the barmaid's eye and I pushed against a boy stood at the bar, spilling some of his beer." Doc indicated using his thumb and forefinger that it had been a pathetically small amount of spillage. "Course, no doubt to impress his arsehole mates, he demanded a replacement beer! And I naturally told him ti fuck right off, at which point some pushing and shoving started, and a couple of half-hearted punches were thrown. Course seeing this Banjo comes charging in and one of the arseholes decides to try to halt his momentum by smashing a beer glass and trying ti shove it in his face. I made a grab for his arm but caught the edge of the glass, which sliced a big chunk out my hand; forty stiches and a severe curb on my sex life! But on the plus side, Banjo kept his charming smile, and then punched the boy so hard that he knocked him out cold before proceeding ti take out his mate with a quick jab. The third arsehole tried ti run, so I tripped him up and he threw himself groveling ti the floor. One look at my hand and all the blood, and Banjo just totally lost the rag! Proceeded ti kick the shit out of his head bouncing it off the brass footrest bolted ti the floor. I grabbed a couple of bar towels ti mop up the blood and then got the fuck out before the police arrived and off wi went inti the A&E."

There was silence as we sat and listened to Doc and his graphic tale of violence.

"Aye, it was a real pisser, we'd been having a great night as well up until then, plenty of laughs."

"Aye well it ended up with you in stiches Doc."

"Scully get ti fuck." Doc shook his head with a weary sigh, .

"Aye well, think the road's wet enough?" Robbie held up an empty glass.

"There's cans in the van," I noted, which seemed to provide the incentive to leave.

Once in the van I dug out the last few cans of McEwans Export and passed them around as Donald farted loudly followed by a predictable chorus of complaint.

"Why did you no' go ti the bogs in the bar?" Doc wailed as he opened the window.

"Ocht I was not going in there after Robbie. It was alright taking a piss, I could hold my breath for that long."

"Aye it was pretty bad, Robbie, what the fuck have you been eating?"

Doc put the van in reverse, "Here, I cannae see a thing by the way."

"Is that cause your eyes are watering? Aye, well let's go… onward then," I pointed at the road, "At least we can see what's ahead of us!"

The Vauxhall zipped along the narrow road between the snow banks and I settled back and stretched out my legs as much as the confined space would allow. As the warm air flooded through it turned the interior of the van into a cozy little microclimate.

Donald yawned expansively his eyes looked heavy, embraced by the warm soporific air he drowsily declared, "Hey, we never decided on a Bothy babe!"

This was a favorite pastime the fantasy concept that a supermodel or similar would wish to give up warmth, running water and electricity and other creature comforts for a few days in our very smelly, very sweaty company. Of course, the responses and retorts were immediate and rapid fire.

"Julia Roberts," I suggested.

"Ah, you pick her every fuckin' year!"

"She's classy and ageless."

"Courtney Stodden."

"Who's that Doc?"

"Nineteen-year-old lass we lungs on her like a pearl diver, married to a bloke in his fifties."

"Ocht aye well, she's in then!"

"Oh hey what about Taylor Swift?"

"Aww whit, Robbie yah pedophile!"

"Aye she looks like a hamster…"

"She sings like Alvin the fuckin' chipmunk."

"Ocht here what about Adele; nice and plump, and what a voice."

"Aye right Doughboy, sure she's woolly enough?"

"Ah, feck off ya cheeky bastard."

"Hey Donald, is it still called dogging if you use a sheep?"

"Ocht aye…!" Donald shrugged, "you see the others like to watch."

Robbie changed the topic back to human females. "How about Cheryl Cole,"

"No way, Robbie, she'd need to be gagged, that squeaky voice would drive you nuts! And she'd smother you to death, man, those thing defy most of the laws of Physics and Motion."

"Ocht, what a way to go though eh…"

"Oh hey yon Brazilian with the endless legs that advertises they kinky kegs, Giselle or Heidi Klum?"

"No way Robbie, she's stood us up once already this weekend."

"Ocht, here they are all a wee bit skinny," Donald complained.

"That speaks volumes for you as a person, or should I say pervert!"

"Hey don't use that tone of face with me , I happen to like a bit of flesh!"

"Aye as long as it's covered in wool."

"Ocht, feck off you."

"If only they knew, they'd be renting out a fuckin chopper ti join us for the smell of Robbie's socks," Doc suggested.

In the silent pause at the end of this game, and before the inevitable happened and the Rolling Stones request was barked from the driver's seat, I tried to see if I could find the news. As I fiddled with the radio, it suddenly found a strong signal and burst into life, just as the chimes sounded for nine o'clock.

We barely listened to the usual litany of national and international disasters before the announcer solemnly declared,

'Police have just confirmed that two hikers killed on Saturday afternoon in a fall on Ben Alder were both from England. We go now to our Scottish correspondent Brian Burke.'

An expectant hush fell upon the van, I held my breath and strained to hear as the signal rose and fell.

'Yes Michael, thank you, following on from our recent report more details have now emerged. The two deceased were in a party of six from Saint Andrews University Mountaineering Club, based at Culra Bothy.

According to reports from surviving members of the party, the two less experienced opted not to climb in low cloud and poor visibility, and instead take a short hike...'

There was a chorus of groans as the signal faded into a static crackle but it returned strongly just as I reached to turn the volume to its maximum.

'...at Ben Alder. Now, some of our hillwalking listeners may be aware that Saturday actually saw a spectacular temperature inversion over most of central Scotland. It would appear that as the cloud cleared, the two opted to summit Ben Alder, but must have strayed close to the edge, falling through the cornice some eight hundred feet to their deaths. The four other members of the party, who were climbing on the North face of the mountain witnessed the fall, and walked out to alert rescue services. Efforts by the Lochaber mountain rescue service to recover the bodies were hampered...

I stared at the radio baffled by what I was hearing then we all groaned again as the signal faded, but this time as it returned, Doc slowed to a halt. The road was deserted anyway, and we sat in silence. The headlights briefly pierced then dissipated into the inky dark Perthshire countryside.

...and low visibility in driving snow today. However, police have just confirmed that the deceased were a man and woman in their twenties from the London area. They are not releasing names until next of kin have been informed.

There were several soft gasps followed by 'shush' as we all strained to hear the undulating signal.

Thank you, Brian; and tell me, you say conditions were ideal?
Yes, the weather on Saturday does not appear to have been a factor. The accident happened in the afternoon, and conditions were reportedly perfect. The cornice on Ben Alder is a notorious spot, and well known for its danger; it would appear that sadly the two novice climbers were not aware of the risk.
Thank you, that was our Scottish correspondent Brian Burke. Now in other news, the leader of the Opposition...

I hit the off button; you could have heard a pin drop, the silence was total. We were all numb with shock, eyes wide as we silently digested the information. The words from the report seemed to echo though the van. I felt nauseous as I repeated the information and struggled to comprehend. "Eh wait a minute man *and a woman* from the London area... but wait he said *Saturday?*"
"So what Sarah said an all!"
"And Mhari."

"How the fuck? That makes no sense!"

"Ocht here but Liz and Rupert said the other four were *all* guys and from Yorkshire."

Again, there was confused silence as the information was mulled over and ruminated upon.

"Here do you think we missed something there, as the signal faded out?"

There was no reply, Doc silently slid the van into gear and we began to move slowly along the darkened road.

"Ocht hey here, eh... I never saw their packs at the Bothy!"

"Eh... what are you on about Robbie?"

"They just appeared, went inti the other room, gone in the morning before we'd got up... Did anyone even hear them leave?"

"Ocht, for feck sake, they never made a sound and left no footprints."

"Naw naw, wait, Donald, we saw their packs!"

"Aye, almost totally buried in snow," Donald stared, suddenly his eyes grew wider, "ocht fer fuck... like they could have been there for over a day, Scully!"

"Saturday, they said they fell on Saturday, Saturday afternoon. Well here, never mind who was in the Bothy on Saturday night... who the *fuck* was that on the *hill* today, the mystery hiker who led us to safety?"

My question was again met with silence. Mind and heart racing, I stared out into the darkness and shook my head.

Again, there was a long thoughtful silence, finally Robbie spoke. "It must have been the same hiker who told them to go to the Bothy; said they'd like it there! What was it Liz said? 'Thank you for making us feel so very much at *home*.' Oh fer fuck, do you mean I was telling a ghost story to a pair of *ghosts*?"

"We *all* were," Donald slurped his beer noisily, shivered briefly and stared silently out the window. "Ocht well, at least we entertained them!"

"Hang on though," I turned to Donald, "were they no' *drinking* the whisky?"

"Ocht aye but no' much right enough, I just assumed it was 'cause they were English."

"Aye but here, *can* ghosts drink?"

After a thoughtful pause Robbie noted, "well if they *can* then the afterlife is no' looking so bad but I've no' exactly seen many ghost in *my* local!"

"Here maybe its the Bothy! Feck, Banjo always did call it the Hotel Caledonia, here maybe he *knew*!"

"Knew what?"

"Ocht that the Bothy had some sort of...." Donald waved his hands as he sought the right words.

I glanced at Doc who had remained silent during the discussion not even his usual cynical snorts, he had just frowned darkly while staring straight ahead.

Donald started to speak again but his voice cracked, so he stopped and slurped his beer, "ocht well then I guess that's the Bothy for you heh… more ghosts, just more feckin' ghosts. Now then, Scully, could be some of the weirdness is starting to make sense? Some of the stranger sightings over the last couple of days perhaps… explained?"

"Aye maybe but who was the mystery hiker and the hooded man, eh? Was it the same guy by the fire as on the Ben…?"

"ACHT…" Doc cut me off, I half expected a dismissive sneering put down as he told us all how stupid we were. Instead, his comment evoked a ripple of nervous laughter.

"Aye more fuckin' ghosts you reckon, Doughboy? Aye well, it would appear that *one of them* goes by the name of *Banjo!* So that's it settled eh… fer fuck! Pack a bottle *each* next year there is *no* fuckin' way that buried whisky will still be there!"

20 EPILOGUE

The Bothy still stands resolutely on the remote shores of Loch Ericht. It is spartan: no electricity or running water, a granite edifice and a sanctuary from weather that can turn on you like a whiplash.

Today there was a visitor, his head covered by the hood of a red Gore-Tex jacket, illuminated by the weak winter light as it filtered through the small recessed window into the cold empty room.

He picked up the Bothy book, its black cover singed by flames, one corner slightly charred. As he paused to smooth a dog-eared corner, a lopsided grin cracked slowly at the entry scrawled across one page.

July 31, 2002, Eck, Andy and Deek fi' Polmont
Stopped at Bothy on the way through fi' Dalwhinnie, fuckin' soaked!
Nae sign of the ghost - just huners of midges!
We hate fuckin' midges!!!!

Flicking through the years, he scanned the ramblings and musing of assorted scribes. Many had never darkened the Bothy door again, unpleasantly surprised, no doubt, by the conditions and complete lack of any basic amenities.

Suddenly, his hand stopped at an inscription, one made by a group of polar opposites to these dismayed neophytes. An entry made during the harsh months of winter. When the ground was hard as iron, the wind rattled the door like an angry drunken locked-out guest and the lack of midges was one of the few virtues. This group clearly relished the harsh conditions, well equipped to counter it with whisky and camaraderie.

He flipped pages as he sought January's entries; finding each year he ran his finger gently across the names of the attendees. The rollcall of hardy souls who had packed up their gear and trudged in over the long miles through weather that ranged from shit to downright atrocious.

Once more, he flicked quickly back and forth. The pages flapped like the wings of a startled bird then stopped as he ran his finger down the middle, tracing the jagged edge of a ripped out page. Raising his head, he stared out the window into the fading light. An eclectic group of World War II airman and hikers clad in ancient tweeds and a lone youth dressed in fashionable street attire had all gathered exactly seven paces due south of a prominent rock. The group applauded joyfully as a young man who had been vigorously digging, hugged a pretty brunette as he held a litre bottle of whisky aloft.

He reached out and gently touched the burnt remnants of the priming gap, then smiled broadly in a manner that could only be described as a shit-eating grin.

After gently closing the Bothy book Banjo pulled the squeaky door closed behind him.

ABOUT THE AUTHOR

Craig Meggy grew up in Edinburgh where he developed his love for Scotland's mountains at any time of the year. Over the years, he has spent many a pleasant night in Ben Alder Bothy, in company as fine as any a man could wish for.

The Key-Stone of the Bridge is the first book in a planned trilogy. Book Two is called **Sixteen Miles to the Gallon and a Double Bed** and deals with earlier exploits of two of the main protagonists. The final book is tentatively titled **Two Lollipop Sticks and a Rubber Band** and it is about the hazards of growing old.

Craig no longer lives in Scotland but he does return whenever possible to pull on a pack and a pair of sturdy boots, and of course to go looking for buried whisky.